"One of the pleasures of the young is dress-up, imagined time-travel, and participation in events more significant than life has afforded them thus far. All of these elements abound in *All in a Garden Green*. Based on a real castle-like estate house in England and an historical visit by Queen Elizabeth I, the novel's protagonists find themselves in unasked-for adventures that both define and stretch them. And readers will greatly enjoy the ride."

—Daniel Taylor
Author of *Woe to the Scribes and Pharisees*

"Fling together a girl about to leave childhood behind, an ancient house filled with chapels and towers and chambers and hidden staircases, lutes and virginals, Queen Elizabeth I, a wise and knowing mentor, and two huge St. Bernards—and then mix them with the slipperiness of time, and you have this rollicking novel that speeds its way to its nick-of-time ending. This is a playful book, spanning four centuries of a changing language, and undergirded by the lovely certainty that what lies ahead will always be better.

—Gary Schmidt
Professor and Department Co-Chair of English, Calvin College, and author of *Okay for Now*

"*All in a Garden Green* is a journey both real and fantastic. During her family's stay at Hengrave Hall, Erica discovers a portal to England's late sixteenth century. Abruptly, history explodes into fascinating and well-researched detail—altered language, antiquated musical instruments, secret rooms and hidden staircases, even a visit by Queen Elizabeth I. Erica's piano lessons were never like this! The story gives young readers a fresh take on resonances between past and present. Highly recommended."

—Ellen Chavez Kelley
Author and poet

"In an old English manor house a young girl enters into history in a way that entices readers to suspend disbelief and take delight in sharing her journey across time. Skillfully drawing upon his own semester with students in England and upon records of a royal visit to Hengrave Hall, Paul Willis has woven a tale that deserves to be read aloud and enjoyed by adults and children old enough to wonder about time past. Ancient customs, young romance, a courtyard, a moat, a mysterious nun, and two St. Bernards are only a few of the features that give this story its singular charm."

—Marilyn McEntyre
Author of *Caring for Words in a Culture of Lies*

ALL IN A GARDEN GREEN

ALL IN A GARDEN GREEN

~Paul J. Willis~

ALL IN A GARDEN GREEN
A Novel

Copyright © 2020 Paul J. Willis. All rights reserved. Except for
brief quotations in critical publications or reviews, no part of this
book may be reproduced in any manner without prior written
permission from the publisher. Write: Permissions, Wipf and Stock
Publishers, 199 W. 8th Ave., Suite 3, Eugene, OR 97401.

Slant
An Imprint of Wipf and Stock Publishers
199 W. 8th Ave., Suite 3
Eugene, OR 97401

www.wipfandstock.com

HARDCOVER ISBN: 978-1-7252-5497-8
PAPERBACK ISBN: 978-1-7252-5496-1
EBOOK ISBN: 978-1-7252-5498-5

Cataloguing-in-Publication data:

Names: Willis, Paul J.

All in a garden green : a novel / Paul J. Willis.

Description: Eugene, OR: Slant, 2020

Identifiers: ISBN 978-1-7252-5497-8 (hardcover) |ISBN 978-1-7252-
5496-1 (paperback) | ISBN 978-1-7252-5498-5 (ebook)

Subjects: LCSH: Time travel -- Juvenile fiction. | England -- Juvenile
fiction. | Country homes -- England -- Juvenile fiction.. |Great Britain
-- History -- Elizabeth, 1558-1603 -- Juvenile fiction.

Classification: PS3573.I456555 A45 2020 (paperback) | PS3573.I456555
(ebook)

Manufactured in the U.S.A.   06/17/20

This book is dedicated

to the memory of

Elizabeth Suzanne Delaney Hess

whose name is

as she often told us

a perfect line of iambic pentameter

Contents

Chapter 1

To Be in England

"WHY DO WE HAVE TO GO?" WAILED Erica. It was August, and hot. Erica was slumped across the piano, her auburn hair mopping the keys. She was supposed to be practicing for her last lesson at four o'clock.

"I've told you," her mother said patiently. "Your father would be lonely without us. And really, dear, it's a wonderful opportunity for the whole family."

Deep down, Erica knew her mother was not an unkind person. Yet she dreaded that word *opportunity*. It always seemed to mean something like soccer camp or a tour of the California missions.

"You have no idea how beautiful the cathedrals are in England, sweetheart."

To Erica, this only proved her point.

"And we'll be living in a manor house—Hengrave Hall—practically a castle. Professor Adams in your father's department says it is just fascinating, and he's been there three different semesters with the students so far."

"Why can't he make it four, then?" Erica said. "If he likes it so much."

"Erica Emily Pickins," said her mother. "It is time to finish practicing."

"Why?" she said. "I won't be taking lessons at Hengrave."

"No, but you can play on the grand piano there in the great hall if children are allowed to use it—we'll ask the nuns for their permission. And you'll want to keep your skills up for when we come back. Music is your talent, Erica. You know how much your father likes to hear you play."

Erica made a repulsive face and folded her arms. "If I'm going to England," she said, "I'm not playing any piano while I'm there. That's final."

What was final about it was the disaster that her last recital had been. But before her mother could touch upon that tender subject, a golden retriever plunged into the living room, pursued by Walter, Erica's brother. The dog paused by the upright piano, panting and grinning. Its tail went *whack whack whack* against the bench. Erica scratched him under the chin and Walter tackled the dog from behind. "Gotcha, Stars!" Walter shouted. Stars was the dog's name.

"Walter," said his mother, "we just had the rug cleaned yesterday, and I've told you to keep Stars out. We've got to keep the house looking nice for the renters."

"Are they going to watch Stars for us, Mom?" Walter said. He gave his dog a full-body hug and hung on, his red hair mingling with the rusty coat of the retriever.

"Yes," she said. "You know that, Walter."

"But why can't we take him? Couldn't we take him? Please? I'd keep him quiet. I wouldn't let him bark on the plane."

"And Stripes too," Erica said. "I could take Stripes." As if summoned by name, a gray-striped cat leapt off the couch and jumped into Erica's lap.

"No," said their mother. "We've been over this." She separated Walter from Stars and chased the dog into the kitchen, then stood wearily in the archway.

"But who are we going to play with, then?" Walter said. He was now writhing on his back on the floor. "Stars and Stripes will be lonely without us, and we'll be lonely without them."

"And all my friends at school," said Erica. "Do you realize I'll be missing half of the eighth grade? When I get back, no one will even remember my name!"

"Erica, you know perfectly well that Dr. Lopez is bringing her children along as well. Pedro is just your age, and Katrina is not that much younger than Walter. I'm sure you'll become best of friends."

"Hah!" said Erica.

"Double hah!" Walter said. "I saw Pedro at the department picnic. He couldn't even hit a softball."

"He's stuck up," Erica said. "And Katrina's a baby. The whole time she'll probably want to be playing with *dolls*."

"They don't play softball at Hengrave Hall from what I've heard," their mother said. "But they do play lots of croquet, and I'm sure you'll all be good at that. And I don't think there will be any room for dolls in our luggage, so don't worry, Erica. You may even get to know some of the students who will be with us."

"The whining English majors?" said Walter.

"Most of them are very nice, I'm sure," said their mother.

"That's what Dad calls them," said Walter. He paused a moment. "Mom, what's an English major?"

"You don't know?" Erica said, not knowing herself, really.

"An English major," said their mother, "is a college student who reads old books written in English—or in England, perhaps—which is why we're all going there, to see where these wonderful books were written."

Walter let this sink in. "That's all?" he said. "I'd have a better reason, if I was going."

"But you *are* going," Erica said. "You have to. That's your reason."

For Erica, though, to judge by the way she pounded out the scales and airs and madrigals when her mother insisted she must get back to practicing, this was not reason enough. When her father came home, long after her loathed lesson, she would have appealed to him as well except that she saw how tired he was. He stood in the kitchen without setting down the briefcase he always carried and spoke on and on in a weary voice about plane reservations and layovers and cancellations and book orders. Also about what he called the curriculum. Apparently, he and Dr. Lopez did not see eye to eye on what they would teach the whining majors. It occurred to Erica that her mother might be the only one in their family who really wanted to go to England. And maybe even *she* was faking it.

After supper Erica went to her bedroom to think about what she would pack the next week. Her father had said it would rain a lot, and that hardly anyone wore shorts. She wanted to bring her baby-blue denim shorts anyway, the ones she had just bought in July with her first babysitting money. They came with matching blue suspenders. She wondered how Pedro would like them, and then wondered why she should care. It didn't matter. He was stuck up. Most boys were, she had noticed.

But, even apart from Pedro, the idea of spending the next four months with just her family and a couple dozen college students in a rundown manor house supervised by a huddle of nuns—very old nuns, she had heard, and likely very crabby ones—well, she could think of better things to do. Like go to the beach with her best friends, just as she had all summer long, whenever her mother had seen fit to unchain her from the piano.

Not that all her practicing had done any good. At last week's recital in a stifling hall at the college, she had played beautifully until all of a sudden, halfway through the Beethoven sonata, her memory had packed its bags and flown to Hawaii, leaving Erica with her fingers poised above the keys and her eyes turned helplessly to her very stern piano teacher, Mr. Macready, who stared back mercilessly. Finally, amid a few titters from the other young performers in waiting, he walked up to where she was sitting and placed the score in front of her. Mr. Macready stood over her as she stumbled to a miserable finish, turning the pages mechanically as if he wished that he were in Hawaii himself. When Erica had mangled out the last chord, she arose stiffly and, turning her back to the audience, curtsied to the other pianists on the stage.

"No," hissed Mr. Macready. "Face the other way, Erica."

But it was too late. This time laughter came not only from the assembled performers but also from the parents behind her.

She had just reprised this scene again, clutching her baby-blue denims in shame, when her bedroom door opened slowly.

"Yours too," Walter said, and stuck out his tongue. He was standing in the hallway just to annoy her.

"My what?"

"Your reason. You have to go just as much as I do."

"That's what you think," Erica said.

"What do you mean?"

"Nothing a little fourth-grader would understand, that's what I mean."

"Hah!" said Walter.

"Double hah!" Erica said. "And get out of my room. It's time for all the fourth-graders to go to bed."

"Make me," said Walter, stepping forward.

Erica rushed at him, nails extended, and he went running down the hall. "And stay out!" she shouted.

Then she slammed the door behind her and lay face-down on the bed. And sobbed. After a while she groped under her pillow and found the Raggedy Ann doll that she still kept hidden there, worn and eyeless. She clutched it to her face until the doll was wet and her cheeks were dry—as if Raggedy Ann herself had taken on her sorrows. She held the damp doll in her hands, kissed it firmly, and realized she would have to leave it here in her bedroom. What a long autumn it was going to be.

"Erica," came a voice behind her. "Are you alright, honey?"

It was the voice of her father. She hadn't even heard him enter. Erica stashed Raggedy Ann back under her pillow and slowly sat up on her bed. Her father was standing with one hand on the doorknob, the other stroking his stubbly chin.

"Your mother said you were upset. About our going to England."

"A little," she said, sniffling. "Don't worry about it, Dad. Don't worry about me."

"But I do, sometimes," he said.

This pierced her with a sliver of comfort. Her father always looked worried, but it was news to Erica that some of the worry was for her. "Really," she said, "you don't need to. You don't need to worry. It's nothing."

Her father stopped stroking his stubble but started to twist the doorknob back and forth. It squeaked a little.

"You're making the doorknob squeak, Dad," Erica said.

"So I am," he admitted, and pulled his hand away.

"Dad," she said, "how are you feeling—about our going?"

"Well," he said, and his gaze went flying off into the corners of her room.

"Well?" she said.

"Well, it will be a challenge," he said. "All those students. Living in a retreat center. With all those nuns. But it doesn't matter how I feel. The department wants me to go, so we need to go. We'll try to make the best of it. We'll try to make it the best trip ever."

"But it does matter, Dad."

"What matters?"

"How you feel."

He looked at her then, strangely and sadly. And closed the door behind him.

CHAPTER 2

Shakespeare Is Dead

"I HOPE WE DON'T HIT ANYONE IN THIS bus," said Walter. He was sitting just behind the driver, who wore a mustache and a uniform. The driver had been completely silent for two hours.

"It's a coach, not a bus," said Pedro beside him. The older boy was dark-haired and golden-skinned, with wire-rim glasses that gave him a superior look.

"Whatever it's called," Walter complained, "someone should tell this guy he's driving on the wrong side of the road."

"The left side, not the wrong side," Pedro said. "The left side is the right side over here."

"Oh yeah?" said Walter.

Erica leaned over the seat from behind him and pinched his arm. "Don't be such a tourist," she said. "If you'd been here before, like Pedro has, you'd know these things."

Pedro gave her a quick, shy glance before going back to the book in his hands. It was called *A Brief History of England*. Erica thought this must be a joke, since it was one of the thickest books she had ever seen.

"He's been here before alright," said Walter. "He's told us ten times already."

"It was only a week," Pedro said apologetically, looking up from his book again. "And I've never been to Hengrave."

"Did your sister come too?" asked Erica. She glanced back at Katrina, who was sleeping on her mother's lap two seats behind.

"She was too small. Just Father and I."

He did not say *my dad and me*, the way she would have. Or *me and my dad*, for that matter. She couldn't decide if the way he talked was pitiful or impressive. She wondered where his father lived, but decided not to ask. Her mother had said he was a native of Mexico, unlike Mrs. Lopez, who was as American as can be—and as pale as a picket fence. Mr. Lopez was also a professor, like his wife, but he taught in another town—another state, even. Erica couldn't remember which one.

"We stayed mostly in Stratford-upon-Avon," said Pedro. "For Shakespeare."

"He wanted you to stay there? Why?" said Walter.

"Who? My father?"

"No, Shakespeare."

"Shakespeare is dead," Erica hissed, thrusting forward and shoving Walter toward the window. Her face was now right next to Pedro's. She was finding him less stuck up than she'd thought.

"What plays did you see?" she asked—not that she knew too many herself.

"A very fine production of *Cymbeline*," Pedro answered. The way he said it sounded British, like the airline steward who had given them peanuts off and on during the night. Now it was afternoon, but to Erica it felt like the morning after a sleepover at someone's house.

Walter turned back to his sister and said, "A very fine production of *Cymbeline*. Very fine indeed, yes." He tucked in his chin and puffed on an invisible pipe.

Pedro ignored him. "Also *The Taming of the Shrew*."

Walter blew his invisible smoke into Erica's face and said, "Yes, yes of course. Jolly good. Jolly good show."

"The taming of the shrimp is what we need," said Erica to Pedro. She thought she saw the ghost of a smile on his serious face.

Katrina started crying behind them. She had woken up and asked for another lemon drop, which her mother said she could not have, since the coach was nearly to Hengrave. "Hush, Katrina," Mrs. Lopez said. "Don't fuss." She sounded tired and embarrassed.

The college students, who were scattered up and down the coach, pretended not to notice. Erica saw that most of them were wearing headphones and couldn't have noticed anyway. A boy in the back stopped playing his guitar and then started again, singing louder as if to cover the sound of the child. "Knock, knock, knockin' on heaven's door," he sang. He kept knock-knock-knocking until they arrived at the iron gates of Hengrave Hall.

The coach had been traveling a narrow highway hedged with fields. It slowed for a shady bend by a wood, passed a group of thatched houses, and turned in between tall stone gateposts, narrowly missing each one.

"Nice work," said Walter to the driver. The driver did not say thank you.

Erica saw a snug cottage set in the woods beside the gate—a gatekeeper's cottage, she decided. Across from it was a small gray lake behind a row of evergreens. She glanced at Pedro nervously. He had closed his book and was looking carefully at the lake.

"There used to be a moat, you know."

"A moat?" said Walter. He was genuinely interested.

"Around the house. Now just this fishpond. That's what Dr. Adams said—the last time he came for tea."

"For tea?" said Walter, wrinkling his nose.

Erica was about to say something especially nasty to her brother when the coach pulled out of the trees. Suddenly there was the house itself, just across an open lawn. It was very tall and stony gray; the front of it seemed to go on and on to either side, a weathered wall capped with ornamented towers. There was ivy covering parts of it, but not much.

"Whoa," said Walter. "Some castle." For once, he sounded truly impressed.

"Strictly speaking, it's not a castle," Pedro said. "It's a sixteenth-century manor house. The battlements and former moat were strictly for show, not at all for defensive purposes."

"It looks like a castle to me," said Walter. "You wouldn't call it the little house on the prairie, would you?"

The coach came to a full stop before great wooden double doors. They were so tall that a smaller door was cut into one of them. This door-within-a-door swung open, and out stepped an old nun, slightly bent. She was wearing a purple habit, almost the same color as the awful dress that Erica's mother had made her wear for their long night and day of travel. A wimple surrounded the woman's face and covered all but a few strands of white hair. She waved at the driver and stood waiting for them to descend while the doors of the coach hissed open. How bright and lively her eyes were, Erica thought.

They seemed to be looking just at her, with a question.

CHAPTER 3

At the Back of the Hall

"WON'T YOU COME INSIDE?" SAID
the nun.

They had all gotten off the coach and extracted a small mountain of luggage from dark compartments underneath. The students started to shamble in, but Pedro hung back, looking up at a maze of carvings that stretched above the double doors. Erica drifted to his side. She followed his gaze and made out a series of crowns and shields and lions and unicorns. Underneath was lettering in strange script. She couldn't have read it even if it were in English, which it wasn't.

"Latin," said Pedro. "I think it says—yes, it does—that the hall was built by Thomas Kytson, in the year of our Lord 1538."

Kytson, thought Erica. She felt a little jolt inside her. That was her mother's maiden name.

"Correct," said a woman's voice beside them. "Can the young lady read Latin as well?"

It was the old nun in the purple habit. All the others had gone inside. Her peculiar eyes were resting upon Erica, just as they had before.

"Not at all," Erica said. But wanting something to say for herself, she quickly added, "I can read music, though."

The face of the nun seemed to soften. "Hengrave is a wonderful place for that," she nodded. "For Latin and for music both." The afternoon sun lit up her chin and ruddy cheeks, and the nun seemed to lapse into contemplation.

Erica felt very tired. The moment seemed to linger, lengthen, and capture itself, as if time had stopped. She was almost content not to say anything else, but finally she did.

"I'm Erica," she volunteered sleepily.

"And Pedro," said Pedro.

"You may call me Sister Julian," the nun said softly, as if not paying them any attention.

"Have you been here long?" Erica asked.

"All day," said Sister Julian.

"I mean, over the years."

"Oh yes," she said. "A long time. A very long time— just like yourself."

"Me?" said Erica. "But I just got here. We've just been here twenty minutes."

"Well," said Sister Julian. "A day, an hour, four hundred years. What really is the difference? In a house like this, you start asking yourself these things."

Erica thought this rather odd, and was going to ask her what she meant when Walter, who had disappeared inside with her parents, came bursting out the door again. "Erica! You've got to see this. You've got to come see this."

"What?" she said, a little annoyed, but too tired to really express it.

Instead of answering her outright, he grabbed her arm and pulled her under the stone arch and through the thick wooden doors. Pedro came along behind. She found herself in a very dim entranceway and then in a hallway leading both right and left. There were tall windows across this hall which gave onto a chill stone square completely surrounded by the building.

"Is that what you wanted to show me?" she asked. "The courtyard?"

Walter shook his head impatiently and pulled her left, down the hallway. Where it angled around the courtyard she saw into a sunny chamber where the students were sitting with their luggage. Her father was saying, "Before assigning your rooms, we're going to take just a moment to let Sister Julian tell us about the rules here, and perhaps some of the history of Hengrave Hall, so that we can"—but Walter kept hurrying her down the hall, and the sound of her father's voice faded. Behind them she saw Pedro and Sister Julian step into the sunny chamber, and heard something like polite applause.

The darkened hallway now opened into a curtained room at the foot of a grand stairway. At the bottom of the banister was a thick wooden ball the size of a globe. Back in the shadows, dim portraits of somber men seemed to ask them why they were not back with the others.

"Walter," said Erica, "can't you show me whatever it is later?"

"Almost there," he panted, and pulled her through a red curtain into a gigantic room with a high-beamed ceiling. On her left was a stone fireplace much taller than her head, and on her right a two-story window that looked onto the courtyard. It was full of bits of colored glass—more shields and unicorns. What most caught her attention, however, was a huge ebony grand piano, standing alone on the polished wood floor.

"Mom told me about this," she said. "You didn't have to drag me all the way here to see it. Now let go."

"Not yet," he said, and whisked her across the great room to a small door and into another hallway again that seemed to be leading to the back parts of the manor. She smelled warm bread and chicken broth, and heard clatter and voices from a kitchen. At last, after descending and climbing a few stairs, they opened a door onto a bright alleyway by a grassy orchard. Walter let go her hand and took off running through the trees. Soon he disappeared through a small gate in a brick wall.

"Come back!" she called. She stood on the pavement uncertainly, then slowly stepped onto the grass. The leaves of the trees were dark green in the late summer, and the afternoon light was warm and full. It occurred to her to forget about her silly brother and to lie down like a dropped fruit and take a nap. Before she could sink to the grass, however, Walter reappeared through the wall, bounding back with enthusiasm. And bounding behind him were two of the largest dogs that Erica had ever seen.

"They're St. Bernards!" Walter shouted. "They live here! Edward says we can play with them! Whenever we want!" Just before reaching her, he sprawled in the grass and the two dogs pounced on him, rolling under and over until they were stretched on their backs. "They want to be scratched," Walter said. "Just like Stars."

The dogs were white underneath, and a mottled chestnut on their sides. Erica picked the nearest one and stroked its chest, then scratched it under the ears. Soon she had buried her face in its furry neck, smelling grass and sky and almost autumn and—well—England, she thought.

"Oh, Walter," she said dreamily. "I *so* like them. I really like them. But what are their names? And who's Edward?"

"Aye, they be likin' you, Miss," said a voice.

Erica looked up from her dog and saw a man in drab brown clothes. He was holding a rake.

She stood up promptly and brushed off her dress. Nervously she put out her hand. "I'm Erica. Walter's sister."

Instead of taking her hand, he patted her elbow with rough calloused fingers. She smelled fresh earth, and tobacco.

"Edward," he said. "I'm the man of this house, you might say."

"The owner?" said Walter.

"No," he laughed, a low chuckle. "The gardener to these twelve sisters here. Sisters of the Assumption, they be. And I can tell you what the assumption is—that I be takin' care of the place. And if I don't, no one does, is the way it is. Not even Meg and Mary here are much to help, but they keep me company, they do."

"I could help," Walter said. "I could help feed 'em."

"That you could, lad. That you could. Carry the scraps out from the kitchen."

"Could I?" said Walter. "Which one's Meg and which one's Mary?"

"Erica's makin' acquaintance with Meg. She's got the white on her forehead. You've got Mary, lad."

"At home," he explained, "we've got Stars and Stripes."

"Oh, that I know," Edward said. "But not much to the Union Jack."

"Who's Jack?" said Walter.

Erica had a vague feeling she needed to put in a word for her country, but couldn't think what to say. Meanwhile, she heard the back door to the manor open behind them.

"Walter! Erica! We've been looking all over for you." It was their mother. After flying all night from America and riding the coach to Hengrave, she looked and sounded bedraggled and exasperated.

"Mom!" said Walter. "We have friends! Meg and Mary—and this is Edward!"

Edward tipped his cap, and their mother gave him a thin smile. "Pleased," he said.

"You can see your friends later," she told them. "But I want you up in our room now. I don't want you running off like this."

"Our room?" said Walter. "Where's our room? Can the dogs come too?"

"Nay, lad," Edward said. "These two girls be outside the hall with me."

Their mother gave Edward a warmer smile.

"Well," said Walter, getting to his feet. "See you later, Meg. Later, Mary. Tomorrow, first thing."

"First thing tomorrow," their mother said, "you two have school."

CHAPTER 4

The Wilbye Chamber

FTER SUPPER, ERICA AND HER FAMILY slept in a high-ceilinged room with wooden shutters her father folded across the windows. In the morning Walter folded them back. The glass panes were streaked with rain, and tall shrubs in the garden below were bending in steady gusts of wind.

"Bummer," said Walter.

Though quite sleepy from their travels they crept downstairs for breakfast and soon after began school. It worked like this. Their father and Mrs. Lopez met with the college students in a corner chamber upstairs, next to the bedrooms. It was called the QE Chamber. When Walter asked why, their mother told them Queen Elizabeth had once slept there.

"Who's she?" said Walter.

"That's why we are having school," his mother said—"to find out these kinds of things."

Katrina and Pedro and Walter and Erica were gathered around her in a small library underneath the QE. The plan was for each of them to work on their lessons till lunchtime, which was not until one o'clock. Mrs. Pickins said they could explore the manor afterward, which Erica was eager to do.

But Pedro was looking irritated. "Queen Elizabeth," he announced to Walter, "was the greatest monarch in English history."

"A monarch?" said Walter. "I thought that was some kind of butterfly."

Pedro and Erica rolled their eyes. Mrs. Pickins opened a book and showed them a picture of a pale woman in a high-cut ruff and voluminous skirt. Four strands of pearls hung from her neck to her waist.

"Oooh," said Katrina, grabbing at the book with sticky hands. "Pretty dress."

"Well," said Walter, "she sort of looks like a butterfly. With that collar she could pretty much float away."

To Erica the woman in the picture looked proud and stern. Her eyebrows arched in a menacing way. "Did she have anyone's head cut off?" she timidly asked.

"Many," said Pedro. "It wasn't safe to cross her."

Erica shuddered.

While she reviewed the factoring of binomials and the proper use of prepositions all that morning, Erica could not get the picture out of her mind. It seemed that the Queen was looking over her shoulder at her exercises. Whenever she made a mistake in her answer a thin high voice said, "Off with her head!" By one o'clock the ax had fallen a dozen times.

When her mother finally let them go, the four of them hurried out across the room with the grand piano (the great hall, Pedro called it) to find out what the nuns and their helpers had made for lunch. It was simply awful. Cooked carrots—and not just steamed but boiled for hours—and a huge cheesy casserole made with a slimy vegetable that none of them had seen or heard of—not even Pedro. Leeks, they were called. When Mrs. Pickins joined them, she said this was a wonderful opportunity to sample the foods of another culture. But she ate very little of the casserole herself, and all that the children could stomach was the bread and butter. They did not even like dessert, a custard that tasted like day-old gravy.

"All the more for Meg and Mary," Walter said. But he was trying to make the best of it.

What made matters worse was that just as the four of them were leaving to explore the manor, Mrs. Pickins remembered that Erica needed to practice the piano. "Sister Julian told me this morning she was happy to learn you are musically inclined, Erica. She says you are welcome to use the piano for the hour after lunch each day. I told her how grateful you would be, and what a splendid idea we all thought that was."

"But Mom," said Erica, "I didn't bring any music." It was true. At the last minute, she had slipped it out of her suitcase and back into the piano bench at home.

But instead of scolding her, Mrs. Pickins merely said, "Sister Julian assured me they have plenty of music which you can use. Some of it was even composed right here at Hengrave, hundreds of years ago."

As for Sister Julian, Erica thought, off with her head! If only she had kept her mouth shut yesterday. Why had she bragged that she could read music?

"But Mom," she began again. Erica felt tears coming.

Rain was beating on the windows of the dining room. The college students, who had liked the meal no better than the children, were scattering to their rooms to study, and Walter and Katrina were scampering up a narrow staircase outside the door. But Pedro remained.

"I'll stay with you while you practice, Erica," he simply said. "I'd like to listen."

"You would?" she asked, rubbing her eyes cautiously. She didn't want him to see that she had started to cry.

"Would that be all right with you?" The way he said it, standing there so tall and thin and bespectacled, was, face it, pretty endearing. Suddenly, she wanted more than anything to play the piano that afternoon.

"Well," she said, shrugging her shoulders, "if you want to, I guess you can."

When they got to the piano in the empty hall, a stack of music was waiting on the bench. Pedro turned on a lamp for her and then retired to a seat in an alcove underneath the huge bay window that looked out on the stone courtyard. The window was covered with coats of arms in stained glass, and on one of them was written the words *Bon temps viendra*. She noticed this because she had seen the same words on the mantel over the dining-room hearth. Erica would have to ask him what they meant. For now, however, she took her place at the keyboard and picked up the top sheet of music.

"I know this one," she said with surprise. "It's the madrigal I was learning at home, 'All in a Garden Green.' Except it looks—so much older."

Pedro came over. "It does look old," he said. The sheet of music was brown and brittle.

"'For two paire of hands,'" read Erica aloud, "'on the double virginalls.' What are virginals, I wonder?"

"I've heard of them," Pedro said, "but I'm not sure what they are. An old-fashioned instrument, I should think. We could look it up."

"Don't bother," she said. "Not now. But look at these notes—so spindly and close together—and each one shaped like a tiny diamond. They almost seem to be drawn by hand."

Pedro peered over her shoulder. "They were," he said. "Can you still read them?"

"I think so. It helps that I sort of know the piece—if it really is the same one."

"Then try it," he urged, and quietly went back to the window, this time lying down on his back on the long stone seat in the alcove.

When Erica put her hands to the keys, a plangent sound filled the room. The piano was perfectly in tune, and as her fingers found the notes they sounded clear and full and sweet, soft or loud as need might be. At first she could hear the rain and wind outside the bay window, but then she heard only the music, one part catching up with the other in madrigal fashion. She wondered how it would sound if someone could play the other two hands with her.

When she finished, she looked over to the seat in the window, but Pedro was gone. Erica sighed. She had possibly played better than she ever had in her whole life, and what had Pedro done? He had left. Just like a boy, she thought.

"I'm right here," Pedro said. His voice came from under the piano. "I wanted to hear the strings close up, and see how they worked."

Erica scooted the bench back and bent under the keyboard. Pedro was lying flat on his back on the hard wooden floor. His legs were crossed and his hands were clasped behind his head.

"You know what?" she said. "You're just about the weirdest person I've ever met. You really are."

Pedro smiled as if she had paid him a compliment. "Play another one," he said. "That was great."

And so she played another, and another, not from the stack of music but from memory, all of the pieces she knew best. Pedro lay contentedly beneath the piano, and Erica felt a sweet delight in having him there, invisible beneath her feet. An occasional student came slouching by with a smart remark, and sometimes a nun came whisking through and gave them a beatific smile. And even her father came shuffling along at one point, her worried and abstracted father, for whom she tried to play extra well. But for the most part they were left to themselves. The afternoon went on and on, the rain kept beating on the window, and the end of the appointed hour came and went. Erica lost track of the time.

She might have played till supper began had Katrina and Walter not come rushing into the other end of the room. There were two matched doors on that end, and over them a balcony. Walter was pointing up to it, breathless.

"There's a chest up there full of costumes!"

"We can dress up!" said Katrina.

"Sister Julian says they used them for costumes in plays when Hengrave was a school or something. And that Edward has the key. Have you seen Edward?"

Erica stopped playing abruptly. "No," she said coldly.

"You've got to help us," Katrina said plaintively. "You've got to help us find Edward."

Pedro crawled out from underneath the piano.

"What are you doing down there?" asked Walter.

"None of your business," said Erica.

"Probably kissing," said Katrina.

Pedro turned red and glared at her.

"Oooh," said Walter. "Erica's got a boyfriend."

"Pedro and Erica sittin' in a tree," said Katrina.

"K-I-S-S-I-N-G," Katrina and Walter sang together. They giggled and ran out of the room. Pedro and Erica heard their voices fade behind the red curtain: "First comes love, then comes marriage, then comes Pedro with a baby carriage!"

"That old thing," Erica said. That song is so *yesterday*. She shook her head. But she was too embarrassed to look at Pedro, who didn't say anything. She put her hands to the keyboard again but somehow the spell had been broken. She didn't feel like playing anymore. There was a long silence, during which they listened to the wind and rain in the courtyard.

"Well," said Pedro as if nothing had happened, "maybe we could explore around a bit."

"Sure," said Erica, sounding perhaps a little too en-thusiastic. Why did everything have to feel so awkward all of a sudden?

She turned off the lamp beside the piano and walked with Pedro to the twin doors that led toward the dining room. Over the left-hand door an inscription read, *Fear God.* Over the right, *Honor the King.* She walked through one, and Pedro through the other, as if they had chosen separate loyalties in life.

"The thing is," Pedro said as they rejoined each other in the hallway, "you can't walk through both doors at once."

"Of course not," said Erica. She looked at him curiously.

"Shall we go up the stair?" said Pedro. It was the same one that Katrina and Walter had climbed after lunch, a little narrow wooden stairway, not at all like the grand set of stairs on the other side of the great hall.

Erica nodded. They picked their way up in dim light, and the floor creaked on the landing. At the top of the stair were three different hallways lined with doors. They chose one that led toward the front of the manor. It was very quiet. On their left, first, was a linen closet. The door was ajar and Erica glimpsed open shelves stacked high with bed sheets and pillowcases.

Across from it was a very small door in the wall with an old black handle. "This must be to the balcony over the great hall," Pedro said. "Or the minstrels gallery, as we should call it."

"The minstrels gallery? What's that?"

"Where musicians would play during banquets in the great hall."

"Is it open?" she said. Then, after a pause, she said, "Wait. How do you even know these things?"

Pedro shrugged and looked at his feet. Erica thought his golden cheekbones flushed a little, and wondered why.

Pedro tried the handle on the door. "Locked," he said. "I guess Edward has the key. Whoever he is."

"Oh, Edward," said Erica. "He's—" She was going to tell him when suddenly they heard giggles and footsteps mounting the stairs behind them. They looked at each other. "Let's hide," she said impulsively. "Then we can jump out and scare them. You get in here. I'll find another place." Before he could agree or object she pushed him into the linen closet.

Just down the hall, through a small archway, was a larger door opposite a window to the courtyard. She flew to open it, noticing over the lintel an inscription that read, *Wilbye Chamber*. The brass knob turned in her grip and the heavy wooden door swung inward.

"K-I-S-S-I-N-G!" she heard just down the hall. Erica was fairly sure that Katrina and Walter had not seen her. She jumped inside and quickly shut the door behind her, breathing hard. In a moment she would leap back out and get them good.

But there was something odd about the floor. She felt as if her feet had landed in long dry stalks of grass, a little like straw in a barn. Slowly she turned and surveyed the room. The floor was strewn with something fresh-cut from the fields. A fire was burning in a grate, and the windows were partially draped with hangings of blue and yellow. Next to the fire was a low, square table, edged with small piano keys.

"Thou art late, Mistress Margaret," said a voice.

She whirled and saw a young man with a small red beard who was seated on a stool in a corner. In his hands he held a fat guitar that looked like a long-stemmed pear.

"'Tis time," said the man, "for thy lesson on the virginals. Thou hast been naught, Mistress Margaret. Thou hast been very naught. And what outlandish clothes thou art wearing."

Erica looked down at her white overalls and pale pink turtleneck. She certainly did not think them outlandish. She looked to see what he had on: a close-fitting jacket, puffy shorts and long tight stockings, all in black. Talk about outlandish.

"How now, Mistress Meg," the man said. "Why starest so unmannerly? Hast thou not seen my new doublet and hose?"

That's when she knew for sure that something strange was happening.

CHAPTER 5

A Lesson on the Virginal

ERICA BEGAN TO PRESS BACKWARD against the door.

"Nay, Mistress Margaret," the young man said, rising to his feet. "Thou mayst not leave. I am not so cross with thee. Master Edward will remain your loving friend and teacher."

She stood stock still, not sure what else she could do.

He strode forward and grasped her hands. "Knowest thou not that your father is riding forth with the Queen on her progress to Norwich—and is soon to return with her train? And knowest thou not that great entertainments are planned, and that you are to perform for her majesty on the virginals—you and your even more wayward sister?"

Erica nodded dumbly as he spoke just inches away from her face. The man's breath smelled terribly rotten, as if he had eaten toasted cheese for weeks on end and never brushed his teeth in his life.

Without waiting for assent or reply, he pulled her across the grass-strewn floor to the low square table and sat her down on a bench before the keyboard. Erica looked at the keys in dismay. They were smaller than those she was used to, and the black keys were especially slender. The entire keyboard extended only a few octaves from side to side. Above them, however, atop the table, was another set of keys altogether. Behind the two keyboards a decorative panel was inlaid, and on it a painting of meadow and forest with human figures romping about. The colors of trees and flesh were brilliant, and a shower of gold seemed to be pouring from the sky into the lap of a beautiful woman in gauzy robes. It was the sort of painting one could almost expect to enter, and Erica felt she might as well. To disappear in a shower of gold would be no less strange than sitting at this instrument.

From a wooden box on a nearby shelf, Master Edward extracted a fresh composition and propped it up in front of the painting. Like the old sheets of music that Erica had just played in the great hall, they were handwritten. But the ink and paper, far from being faded and brittle, were new as could be. The notes and staves were crisp and black, with occasional words penned between in blood-red crimson. The paper was supple, and actually shone.

"We shall try this again, together," said the young man, and he sat on the bench right next to her. Fleas were hopping about on his hose, and Erica did her best to ignore them.

With some effort, she squinted at the music to see if she knew how to start. That is when she saw a familiar direction: "For two paire of hands, on the double virginalls."

"Why, it's the same," she whispered, not meaning to speak aloud.

"Of course it is," said Master Edward. "Thou hast been working on this for a fortnight. 'Tis mine own arrangement of the old ballad—as a madrigal. Today thou wilt play the right-hand part, as always, and after thou art sure of it, I shall bear thy sister's part on the left."

She stared at him in disbelief.

"You may begin, Mistress Margaret," he said peremptorily.

For a moment Erica thought to explain that she had never seen a virginal before in her life (if that indeed is what this was), that she had no idea who Mistress Margaret might be, and that Mr. Macready, her piano teacher, for all his faults and severities, at least used a mouthwash that made his breath smell very nice. Master Edward was making a huge mistake. But she couldn't get any of this out. Instead she found herself placing her hands on the tiny keys. She took a deep breath, just as she had at her last recital, and began to play.

To her surprise, she found at once the proper notes. The sounds that came from the virginal were not the full, rich, resonant tones that had issued from the grand piano. They were higher, and briefer, and almost tinkly, like water drops. Erica nearly laughed aloud. She soon became used to the sound, however, as her fingers flew across the keys, and it came to her mind that the sprightly, spirited music she made was much like that of a harpsichord, which she had heard once or twice on her father's favorite classical station.

And the strange thing was that the second keyboard, mounted above the one she was using, was playing along without being touched, apparently an octave higher. Whenever she touched a key below, the identical key was depressed above her, as if she were being accompanied by an invisible presence that copied every stroke she made. The small keys hopped before her eyes in every direction, just like the fleas that were dancing now on her overalls.

"Splendid," said Master Edward, nodding his head in a way that kept time with the music. "Excellent, young lady. Thou hast improved beyond all measure." He smiled at her with his awful breath, and she played on, gaining confidence as she realized the score did not call for any more notes than were actually present underneath her fingertips. When she finished she gave him a satisfied smile in return, and folded her fingers in her lap, pinching a few fleas on the sly.

"Now," he said, "once more, and I shall join thee." He turned the sheets of music back to the start of the piece. "With feeling."

Without hesitation Erica began again—and instantly she became aware of Master Edward playing with her at her side. There hardly seemed room for him there. Nevertheless the tinkling drops of two hands became a sparkling rain of four, multiplied to a downpour by the echoes of the upper keyboard. She had thought the piece beautiful, but now it was becoming a wonder. She sensed that Edward truly was a master musician, and as note followed note in complexity of counterpoint, Erica became lost again in ebb and flow of melody that filled the room.

And then, suddenly, Master Edward began to sing, in a clear sweet tenor, the words penned beneath the notes.

"*All in a garden green,*" he sang, "*two lovers sat at ease, as they could scarce be seen among, among the leafy trees.*"

He pointed then to the words written underneath her own part, and nodded as he held the end of a measure on a tremor of notes. It felt like the most natural thing to join in, so she did. "*All in a garden green,*" she sang. And he continued, just underneath her, "*two lovers sat at ease.*" His eyes flashed pleasure as he sang in return, and then she replied again, and so on, back and forth, climbing and descending the scales, until they ended in one joined harmony.

Silence came back to the room, the low crackling of the fire, as if it were the final sound of the composition. Erica felt her heart beating, and Master Edward was evidently too pleased for words. Finally he said, "This, Mistress Margaret, *this*, is music. Suddenly thou art so accomplished, so expressive, so nonpareil, so, so—I wonder at it. I marvel, young lady. The Queen will be delighted to hear you—for thou knowest she is a practiced performer on the virginals herself."

He got up and began pacing the room, kicking the stalks of grass away as if they were obstacles in his path. "Now," he continued, "if we could only get thy sister Mary to pay her attention to the work."

He stopped and motioned for her to rise. "Today, for thee, this is enough. Go seek thy sister—ask her to come to me anon."

"Anon?" said Erica innocently.

"Presently," said Master Edward, clucking his tongue like a metronome. "And return tomorrow the same time, at four of the clock. We shall rehearse you both together."

Erica quietly rose from the bench, relieved to have the lesson over before she could gather any more fleas—and before she could be found out for the imposter that she was. If he had set her to another of his arrangements on the virginal, or asked her to play that guitar-like instrument in the corner—the one shaped like a fat pear—she would soon have shown her incompetence. And after having pleased Master Edward so well, it would be a shame to disappoint him.

At the door she turned to bid him goodbye, and even made a little curtsy, though she was not wearing a skirt. She took a last look at the virginal and its curious painting, the little fire, the curtains of bright blue and yellow, and the satisfied music master standing in his new black doublet and hose. Then she undid the latch and slipped back into the hall, closing the door behind her.

She let out her breath, feeling as if she had held it underwater for the past many minutes. Everything looked much the same as when she had left. The white plaster hallway felt a little dimmer, that was all, as at the end of afternoon. Across the way, windows looked down into the damp courtyard. It had stopped raining. She turned through the arch to her right, into the gloomier part of the passage, not knowing what she would find.

"Pedro," she whispered fiercely. His name echoed down the hall. No one answered.

She tried the door to the linen closet, but it was locked. So she crossed the hallway to try the door to the minstrels gallery. Perhaps it would be open now. Yes, it was. The handle turned easily, and the door swung inward. She stooped under the low lintel, and found herself in the steep balcony high over one end of the great hall. Several tiers of dark wood benches dropped away at her feet. Beside her was a little landing. It felt very dark.

"Pedro?" she whispered again.

She heard some movement down the landing to her right, and made herself turn to face it.

"Surprise!" came a collective shout. Three figures leapt from the shadows, arms held high, and Erica screamed. Pressing in upon her were a brown-robed friar, a pirate in a purple coat, and what looked to be a fairy princess. All three of them started laughing uncontrollably, and in that moment she recognized them. Pedro was the tall thin friar, Walter the pirate, and Katrina the little princess.

"What are you doing, scaring me like that?" she demanded.

"Hah!" said Walter, adjusting his coat. "Like you weren't going to do the same thing to us. Where have you been, Erica?"

"Yeah," said Katrina. "Pedro said you were hiding just down the hall, waiting to jump out and scare us—didn't you, Pedro?"

Erica looked at him, feeling a slight sense of betrayal—but most of all, feeling relief that they were all together again. It was good to know she had an obnoxious brother named Walter and not a mysterious sister named Mary—and that Pedro was still here to help her.

He looked back at her shyly. "Where were you, Erica?" he asked.

"I was in—the Wilbye Chamber, I guess they call it. I found—well, I found some musical instruments there, and started to play them. I'm sorry if I took too long."

"What kind of instruments?" asked Pedro. He was clearly intrigued.

"The room just down the hall?" said Walter, interrupting. "There's no instruments in there. Me and Katrina checked it out. Only thing in that room is a few chairs and a TV. You're fibbing, Erica. You were just watching cartoons."

"Not in the room I was in," Erica said.

"Yeah?" said Walter. "Well let's go see." He ducked past her through the door.

She followed quickly. "Walter, I wouldn't go in there if I were you. You do *not* want to go in there."

Pedro and Katrina were right behind her in the hallway. She started to run, but Walter was too far ahead. Before she could catch him, he reached the door to the Wilbye Chamber and threw it open.

"See?" he said triumphantly. Pedro and Katrina crowded around him but Erica hung back. Then Pedro looked back at her sorrowfully.

In spite of herself she peered over his shoulder. She saw a very plain room with dull red curtains, a brown rug, and a gray electric heater against the wall. Where the double virginal had been was an old, dusty television.

CHAPTER 6

Sister Julian's Advice

THE SUN CAME OUT THAT EVENING, but Erica hardly noticed. After a disagreeable supper the others went out to explore the many lawns and gardens, glistening from the new-fallen rain. Erica claimed she was tired and went up to their room. Her mother said it was jet lag. "It takes a few days," she said. "For a while you feel lost in time."

"Yes," said Erica, curled on top of her bed in the corner. "That's exactly how I feel, Mom." But of course that was only part of it. Erica didn't know which was worse: having apparently opened a door on another time or having the others—especially Pedro—think she had told an outrageous lie about what she had found in the Wilbye Chamber. Several times that afternoon she had thought to take him into her confidence. But somehow she hadn't been able to. After all, she could hardly believe what had happened herself.

And then there was the appalling question of whether she should try to return the next day—"at four of the clock," as young Master Edward had put it. Would the door to the past remain open to her? Was she bound by promise? Would the real Margaret put in an appearance and expose her as a visitor from a foreign era? She was surprised to be even entertaining the choice of going back at all. But the music they had played together—played and sung, side by side—had been so achingly beautiful. And the mystery of it. And the chance to perform before the Queen. (Which queen? she wondered.) Master Edward's hopes were so high—she couldn't let him down, could she?

Then an awful thought came. Suppose she did return to the chamber at four the next afternoon. And suppose that the virginal and music master were waiting for her when she entered. Fine, that would be just as before. But what was to guarantee that Pedro and Katrina and Walter would be waiting for her back on this side of the door? What if there were no way to return again? She began to shiver violently and thought of the music master's breath reeking like rotten cheese.

"Are you well, Erica?" asked her mother. She was unpacking the last of their things and putting them away in a bureau.

"I think so," Erica said miserably.

Her mother came over and laid the back of her hand on Erica's forehead. "You feel a little warm," she said distractedly.

"It's nothing, Mom. Don't worry."

"It wouldn't hurt to—oh dear," she said, interrupting herself. "I believe I forgot to pack the thermometer—I know I did. I'll have to go downstairs and see if Sister Julian has—"

"Really, Mom, you don't need to bother her. I'm okay."

But her mother was heading for the door, undeterred. "Mom?" she asked.

Her mother paused in the doorway.

"When did Queen Elizabeth visit Hengrave Hall?"

"I have no idea, exactly, dear. It would have been at least four hundred years ago. You could ask Sister Julian."

"Did any other queens come here?"

"I don't know, Erica. But I'm glad you're taking such an interest in Hengrave—such a rich history, and here we are, right in the middle of it!"

With that she whipped out of the room on her motherly errand, and Erica was left staring after. For a long time she tossed and turned on her bed, trying to pretend she was really ill. That might solve her problem. She couldn't go to the Wilbye Chamber if she were sick.

Erica got up and went into the bathroom in the small round tower off the corner of the chamber. She felt like taking a shower, but there was only a porcelain tub on clawed feet. That's the way it was in England, her mother had said. So she simply stood on the old stone floor and studied her face in the mirror over the wash-basin. She looked pale enough. Certainly there was distress in her eyes. Perhaps she could pass as being a bit under the weather.

Erica returned to the chamber and heard the sound of barking through the windows, which were partly opened. She knelt on her bed and looked outside. Walter and Katrina and the two great St. Bernards were tumbling across the west lawn. Even from her high and distant vantage point, Erica could see that the clothes of the children

41

were soaking wet with grass stains. Beyond them, on an elevated grass plot, the college students were playing an elaborate game of croquet; her father was seated nearby on a low bench, poring over a large book. Edward and Pedro were standing, arms folded, on a gravel walk, as if supervising everyone. Edward was talking and sometimes nodded at plantings in a nearby bed of roses, red and white. Erica was sure that Pedro was taking in every word. It was uncanny, the way Pedro remembered everything he read or heard. Why did he have to be like that? Yet somehow it did not put her off. Not completely, anyway. She recalled the sight of him that afternoon, stretched out attentively beneath the piano, enthralled with the madrigal and completely unconscious of the ridiculous figure he made.

Walter began shouting and running around a mossy fountain in the center of the lawn. The dogs chased him one way, then another, trying to overtake him as he kept changing directions. "C'mon, Meg! C'mon Mary! Can't catch me! Can't! Can't!" Finally the dogs divided to conquer, each choosing a separate route and trapping Walter between them, upending him in a two-way tackle. He went down shrieking with laughter.

But it was the names, not the laughter, that rang in Erica's ears. *Meg? Mary?* Wasn't Meg the name that Master Edward had given her, and didn't he say that Mary was her so-called sister? How strange, she thought. Whom could she ask about it?

Behind her, the door to the chamber opened quite suddenly. Erica turned and sat down on the bed. Across the large room she saw the inquiring eyes of Sister Julian, frail and bent in her purple habit. Mrs. Pickins hesitated behind her.

"Erica," her mother said, "Sister Julian is here to check your temperature. She was a nurse in the war, she says, and we are so fortunate that she is willing to help you."

Erica noticed how exceedingly deferential her mother was to Sister Julian. Was it because they themselves went to a Catholic church at home? Or because they only attended twice a year, Christmas and Easter? Was her mother's respect genuine, or some vague expression of guilt?

The nun slowly approached the window, but Erica's mother stayed by the door. When Sister Julian reached her side she took Erica's hand and nodded back to Mrs. Pickins. "You may leave us for a while, my dear. I should like to speak with Erica for just a few minutes, if you please."

Mrs. Pickins waved cheerily and left. Erica felt abandoned.

The sun was setting through the windows, and Sister Julian's face looked ruddy and bright. The few wisps of white hair that stuck out below her wimple seemed to shine.

"So, Erica," she said, gazing at her carefully, "how is your music getting along?"

"Quite well, thank you," Erica replied, looking down.

"None of us sisters has the skill to play so well as I know you did this afternoon. You were a great delight to all of us."

Erica looked back up, surprised. "You heard?" she said.

"Oh, yes," laughed Sister Julian, letting go Erica's hand. "We all did. It is only the sitting by yourself that makes you feel you are all alone. We are a community here, you know."

At that moment, Erica felt they were all a pack of spies, rather.

"That music," Erica said. "The madrigal that was left for me—it seemed pretty old. Do you know who wrote it? And when? I have played it at home, but my music book says the composer is anonymous."

"I do not know the composer either, but I can guess," said Sister Julian. "The manuscript belongs to the house. It was perhaps written by the great madrigal composer, John Wilbye, who lived in a chamber across the courtyard from this one around the year 1600."

She pronounced the name *will be*—not *will by* as Erica had thought. But that is not what most concerned her. Erica looked out the window at the dogs and children down on the lawn. Then she looked back up at Sister Julian.

"John?" Erica murmured. "Not Edward?"

"Edward?" said Sister Julian, smiling. Then she seemed to remember something. "Yes, Edward. That would be Edward Johnson, resident musician here before John Wilbye, just at the time of the Queen's progress."

"Her progress? What's that?"

"Her summer travels with the court. She went on progress out of London every summer, but only came to Hengrave once, on her return from Norwich, at the end of August, just about this time in fact, in 1578."

"But Edward Johnson," Erica said eagerly in spite of herself. "What do we know about him?"

"Very little," said Sister Julian. "I'm afraid he lies in the shadow of his famous successor. He went to Cambridge. He helped to entertain the Queen for the Earl of Leicester at Kenilworth in 1575. He probably arranged the music for her visit here at Hengrave, three years later. If he were competent and well-liked, he would have had his own chamber, perhaps the one that became Wilbye's."

She looked at Erica curiously. "But what gave you the name Edward, child? So few people know of him. Only scholars of English music, and some of us here."

Erica didn't know what to say. "I'm not sure," she said slowly. "I guess I was thinking of Edward the gardener. He seems kind of musical, right? Or, at least, he seems to belong here."

"Indeed he does belong here," said Sister Julian generously. "But he is one person who does not have a musical bone in his whole body. But for all that, he's named after our old musician, and for all I know descended from him."

"Sister Julian," said Erica, pausing before she could continue. "Why did Edward name his dogs Meg and Mary?"

The nun looked at her cautiously. The sun had suddenly finished setting, and the bright face and white hair were in shadow now. "Because they're his pupils, I suppose," she said. "Just like the daughters of Sir Thomas Kytson the Younger and his wife Elizabeth Cornwallis, who learned their music from Edward Johnson."

"What kind of music?" Erica asked eagerly.

"Mainly the virginal," she said. "Perhaps a little on the lute. But the virginal was considered the proper instrument for young ladies. The lute was more for the boys and men. Perhaps you know that Queen Elizabeth herself was an accomplished performer on the virginal—or the *virginals*, as they called it then. All of her life. She often surprised her courtiers and visitors at the oddest moments.

"But enough," said the nun, taking a small flask from her robes. "I am supposed to be taking your temperature, and here I am rehearsing useless history. I have just made our annual batch of rose-petal wine from the garden, and I have brought you a small sip. Better than any thermometer, and you and I know, dear, that you are not really ill."

Erica felt alarmed and looked down. But after a pause she accepted the flask and took a very tiny drink. It did taste like roses, and gave a hot flush to her face.

"There is a saying in this house," the nun said. "It is written in French: *Bon temps viendra*. Good times will come. It is always so."

So that's what it means, thought Erica. She remembered the words from the mantel in the dining room and the window in the great hall.

Sister Julian brought her face even closer to Erica's in the fading light. "There are prayers," she said earnestly, "that reach across the centuries. We are all one community at Hengrave Hall. We find ways to help each other—to bear one another's burdens—when one of us is in distress. Or perhaps I should say that ways are found. Even across great lengths of time. Do not be afraid, child, to play your music where you may and when you must. My prayers are with you night and day, and I doubt not they will make a way for you to return."

To this, Erica grew wide-eyed, and her hands trembled. She passed back the flask of rose-petal wine, afraid she would drop it.

"No need to say a word, child. Again I tell you, do not be afraid. Perhaps there will be others to join you." Sister Julian enveloped her in a sudden embrace, strong and full for the sagging bones of such an old woman, then just as suddenly let her go.

"Sister Julian," Erica whispered, "what did Margaret Kytson look like?"

"No one knows, my dear. Perhaps much as you do."

"My mother is a Kytson," said Erica.

"That I know," said Sister Julian. "And so are you, deep in your bones. I knew it when I first saw you. Because I am a Kytson too."

"But why should that even matter?" Erica suddenly wailed. She was feeling sucked into a whirlpool of conspiracy—a family conspiracy—that she did not even understand.

"Heaven knows," said Sister Julian. "I certainly don't."

The old nun raised her eyebrows under her wimple. Then she began to shuffle back to the chamber door. Before she got there, Mrs. Pickins knocked and entered, looking curious and innocent.

"Erica is doing well," the nun told her. "A little tired, I should say, and only a slight flush of fever. Just the excitement of getting here, I should suppose. Let her rest and she will be pretty as pink tomorrow, say, by teatime, four of the clock."

The room was dim, but it seemed to Erica that Sister Julian winked at her as she slipped out the door.

CHAPTER 7

The Song in the Chapel

THE NEXT MORNING WAS LONELY FOR Erica. Her mother brought a tray of breakfast up to her and then disappeared downstairs to meet Pedro and the children for school. Her father had been up early reading books and marking papers at a round table in the corner of the room. From the deepening furrow in his brow and the way he was mumbling under his breath, Erica could tell he was not yet enjoying their visit to Hengrave. He did not even go down to breakfast, and when time came for him to teach his class in the QE Chamber, he rushed out the door without even saying goodbye, much less giving her a kiss and needed words of comfort.

What a mystery he was to her. Dutiful to a fault, but always a little sad, it seemed. *Dad*, she always wanted to say, *what's wrong with you?*

For an hour she lay dully in the room by herself. The morning grew, and no one came to check on her. Erica felt quite forgotten. She doubted if anyone would come before lunch. Fine, she thought. She would just get out of bed and explore the manor on her own. Her mother would be downstairs all morning, her father just down the hall. Let them stay there.

She quickly dressed in her baby-blue denim shorts (the ones with matching blue suspenders) and stepped into the hallway. The sun was already shining down into the inner courtyard. She looked through a window across the courtyard to the hallway on the other side, and through its own courtyard window she could see the door to the Wilbye Chamber, right where Sister Julian had said it would be. But Erica wasn't going there yet. Not until teatime, at four of the clock. If the nuns had served tea yesterday, she must have missed it—by just a few hundred years.

She was curious to see the QE Chamber, at the end of the hall on her left, for her father had said it contained an ornate painting of the Queen on the wall. But it was full of college students just now—she would have to wait. She crept to the door anyway and heard her father droning on in a rather unexcited voice about Shakespeare, about comic kinesis in early Elizabethan drama, about doubling of characters and Aristotelian recognition—and much else she did not begin to understand.

Why did he have to sound so dispirited? It worried her. She wished that he could hear her play the virginal with Master Edward.

And right then, just as she was thinking of music to cheer her father, she heard the sounds of singing from the other end of the hallway. They were the voices of women in harmony—slow, soft, mournful notes. She looked but saw no one. How curious, and how lovely. She walked down the hall again, past a couple of student rooms, past the room that Pedro shared with Katrina and his mother, and past the room for the Pickins family. The rooms were marked as the Court, Chintz, Red, and finally Blue Chambers. All the while the singing grew sweeter and louder. It seemed to come from behind a small unmarked door at the very end of the hallway.

Erica stood next to the door for a long while, her hand on the fluted knob. She tried to convince herself it was enough to stand outside and listen. But that weak notion did not prevail. Without really intending to, Erica opened the door a crack and peeked inside. She saw that the door led to a tiny balcony, smaller than the minstrels gallery over the great banqueting hall. This balcony was fitted with a single bench that overlooked a beautiful chapel. Dozens of decorated windows mounted high on the far wall. She would have called them stained glass, but they looked much older and more intricate than any of the stained-glass windows she had seen in America. And she could see the singers as well. Almost a dozen of the nuns were clustered about an altar under the windows, holding their faces up to the reddish light. First one group sang, then another, just as in a madrigal. But this was slower, like a prayer, and did not seem to be in English.

Since their backs were to her, Erica opened the door further and slipped inside, taking a seat upon the bench. If they turned about she could duck down and hide behind the parapet at the front edge of the gallery. Until then she would take in the singing. Sometimes a single nun would lead out ahead of the rest in a clear but quavery silver voice. Erica was fairly sure that this was Sister Julian, standing just in front of the others. There was rich and full comfort in the way she sang, a sense she was repeating the lead of other voices, other times. The singing rose in the brightness of the reddish light, and one seemed to stand for the other; Erica felt that she heard the light, that the voices shone.

When the singing was finished, the nuns all knelt together in silent prayer around the altar, which she could now see was covered with angels carved in the stone. Erica watched and wondered what they prayed for. Then the nuns held out their arms and sang an extended amen, many-layered like clouds streaking the morning sky. When they rose to leave, Erica ducked out of sight, crouching low. She could hear their footsteps tracing the hard floor, the fringes of their habits brushing the wooden pews. A door opened directly beneath her. The nuns swooshed out, and Erica was left in silence.

How utterly beautiful, she thought.

She was just about to rise from her crouch when the door beneath her opened again, and footsteps hurried down the aisle. She supposed that one of the younger nuns had forgotten something and returned. But the footsteps ended at the altar and did not resume. Whoever it was had come to stay. There was silence again in the chapel, broken by the shallow sound of Erica's breath, which she tried to make slow and even. Even her heart seemed loud in her ears. Whoever it was below her made no sound at all.

And then she heard a stifled sob. And then another. The person at the altar was crying. The weeping was soft, but all the more powerful for the way in which Erica sensed it was being held back. She couldn't help wondering who it was, and what was the matter. At the same time the last thing she wanted was to intrude upon someone's private grief.

And then there were more than tears—there were words. Earnest, heartfelt, poured-out—words that carried anguish. "Let it not be. Oh, let it not be," said the voice. "I cannot, I cannot, I *cannot*." And then there came a new burst of sobbing—a wail, really. And Erica was now terribly curious, for the voice she heard was not that of a nun but that of a girl.

The sobbing went on, and Erica at last decided to peek over the edge of the gallery. Trying to make no noise, she raised her head and peered down into the chapel. The ornate windows distributed their clear, reddish light as before. There were the pews, there was the altar—and there on her knees, facing away from her, hands clasped, was a young girl of just about Erica's size—though it was hard to tell, for she wore a wide, hooped skirt of a sort that Erica had never seen anyone wear in her life. The skirt was white, with many tucks and flourishes, and was topped by a tightly cut bodice all robin-egg blue, about the color of Erica's shorts. The girl's dusty auburn hair fell just below her shoulders, pleasant against the blue bodice. It was just the length that Erica had had hers cut before they came. To see the girl cry made Erica almost sorry for herself.

Once again the young girl began to speak imploringly. "Ay me," she sighed. "Ay me, unfortunate me. Let it not be. Let her not come. I cannot. I cannot. I *cannot*."

Perhaps because the girl seemed to be so young—as young as herself—or perhaps because she was so very curious, or even perhaps because she wanted so much to help, Erica found herself suddenly saying, quite out loud, "Excuse me, but what is it you cannot do?"

The girl straightened as if she had been spoken to by one of the angels carved in the stone of the altar. She stopped crying. Very slowly, very stiffly, she turned her head. At first she did not know where to look.

"Up here," said Erica.

The girl stood up and turned completely about, letting her arms drop to her sides.

Their eyes met.

And now it was Erica's turn to shiver. For the upturned face below her was the mirror of her very own.

Chapter 8

Margaret at Last

"I KNOW WHO YOU ARE," WHISPERED ERICA from the balcony. "Your name is Margaret."

The girl nodded cautiously, her eyes wide with astonishment. "There be few here who know not that," she said in a small voice. "But who, pray, are you who look so very like mine own image in the glass? And what brought you to spy upon me here in our chapel?"

Erica rose from her crouched position, and Margaret came a few steps toward the balcony. Each kept her eyes on the other.

"I'm—well, it doesn't really matter who I am," Erica said. "You wouldn't believe me if I told you. But—" She stopped, a new thought occurring to her. "But I suppose I am a cousin of sorts—a distant cousin, many times removed, you might say."

Margaret put her head to one side, as if weighing this claim.

"And I didn't really mean to spy. I just happened to look into the balcony here a few minutes ago to—*um*—hear the music."

The girl in the aisle looked at her sharply, and Erica faltered. "The singing, you know."

She realized she had made a mistake. Of course there had been no singing in the chapel. That was four hundred years in the future. The time must have changed again as the nuns left, when Margaret walked through the door.

"Okay, forget about the singing," said Erica. "What I meant was—what really matters—is that I am sort of a visitor. And—and that yesterday Master Edward—Master Edward Johnson, I believe—the music master—thought I was you, and played with me on the virginal in the Wilbye—I mean, in his chamber just around the courtyard. You see, I came for your lesson by accident, and I guess—well—I guess that you and I look sort of alike?"

A slow, scared smile crept across Margaret's face. "So, 'twas you," she said wonderingly. "Master Edward paid my mother so very many compliments on my playing yesterday. And 'twas to my great astonishment, for all during my lesson I was hidden here in a corner of the chapel, praying for deliverance. And 'twas you, angel or demon or happy genius, that hast delivered me!"

"No, really," Erica said, overwhelmed by this response. "You can just call me Erica. Believe me, I'm no angel or demon. And Pedro's the genius, not me."

"Say what thou wilt, thou hast come in good time, Erica, and I am most happy for it. Come down, come down, if thou beest in the flesh, and let me most pleasantly speak to thee."

Margaret pointed to a tiny circular staircase that led from the edge of the gallery down to the chapel proper.

Erica could have sworn the stairs were not there when she had entered. She climbed down the narrow steps and Margaret met her at the bottom, arms out. Erica joined her hands with Margaret's, and they stood for a long time regarding each other. They were exactly the same height. They had the same dusty auburn hair, the same green eyes, the same slightly upturned nose, the same dimples, the same pert mouth, the same small chin. All that told them apart was their clothing.

"'Tis marvelous," breathed Margaret.

"I agree," said Erica, almost matter-of-factly. "It is amazing." Then she said, "But tell me. What's the matter? Why were you crying?"

When she heard this, Margaret looked almost as if she would cry again. "Would it be a weeping matter—" she began, her voice quavering. "Would it be a weeping matter if thou couldst not play on the virginals, but thy mother and father and music master insisted you play before the Queen, and the Queen were coming this very day, at four of the clock?"

"So soon?" said Erica. "I thought—"

"So thought we all," said Margaret. "But my father returned in haste last night from attending her majesty back on her progress. She will stay no more at Thetford and is bound for Hengrave as we speak. Master Edward is in charge of the entertainments, and he is most beside himself. He thinks that I played so very well for him yesterday that I and my sister are to perform for the Queen in the great hall this very night. At this present hour I am supposed to be practicing with Mary in Master Edward's chamber. And I cannot. I cannot. I *cannot*."

Here the girl really did dissolve in tears once again. Erica let go her hands and put her arms around her.

"It can't be as bad as all that, Margaret," she heard herself say timidly. She thought of what Sister Julian had said to her: *Do not be afraid.* She wished she could pronounce it in just that confident way. But no, she wasn't Sister Julian. She was just Erica, almost as afraid as Margaret crying on her shoulder.

Then she thought of what to do. It was obvious. "Meg?" she said. "I can call you Meg, can't I? Isn't that what everyone calls you?"

Meg sniffed and nodded.

"Meg, if you give me something to wear—some of your clothes—I could play for you tonight in the great hall. If you hurry, I could even practice again with Master Edward in his chamber."

The sniffling stopped. Meg stepped back from her embrace. "Thou wouldst?" she said. "Thou truly wouldst?"

"I don't know about *wouldst*, but I will," said Erica, feeling more brave as she said it. "I'm beginning to think that's why I'm here—to help you."

"And thou truly knowest how to play the virginals?"

"Apparently," said Erica. "Though I've only played it once in my life. But I do know how to play the piano."

"The what?" Meg said.

"The pi—" Then Erica stopped, realizing Meg would not have heard of it.

"No matter," said Meg. "'Tis probably one of those many instruments up in Master Edward's chamber. I cannot remember them apart. He says there never was a girl that had a deafer ear for music."

She looked at Erica gratefully. "But here I am, chattering like a popinjay, when I should be helping you to dress. Come hither, Erica."

And with that she led her back down the aisle to the altar, then over to a panel in the wall on the right, about the size of a cupboard door. It was no different from the many other wooden panels that covered the entire wall. Meg stooped down and ran her hand along the wood, then pushed with her fingers near the corner, just where the beveled panel met the floor. The wood quietly gave way, the entire panel swinging inward. The space beyond was completely dark. There was no telling how large it was, or where it led.

"Our priest hole," Meg confided. "A place to hide our holy fathers from the bloody Protestants."

Erica must have looked somewhat confused.

"And that includes the Queen," she said indignantly. "Just yesterday she imprisoned young Master Rokewood, our dear neighbor in Thetford, and took away Euston Hall as forfeit to the crown. Why? For an image of the Holy Virgin found in his hayrick and burned at the Queen's command. So now he hath lost both land and home for what she so graciously chooseth to call our 'badness of belief.' Those were her very words—my father heard them. He hath an idea she's only come to Suffolk and Norfolk to frighten good Catholic folk."

Erica did not understand all this, but did not ask for explanation. She could tell that it stirred Meg deeply.

"Fortunately," Meg continued, "our two priests are far away at the moment. But don't you see? If the Queen is in any way displeased with her entertainment at Hengrave, the same sad thing could happen to us. The whole parish knows us for a family of the old faith. One nod of her head and off my father goes to prison—and off we go, Hengrave taken away from us, for the rest of our miserable lives."

"The Queen would do that?" Erica asked.

"Most assuredly," said Meg. "Oh, Erica, Erica, Erica. You must play well for me, you must!" And Meg embraced her, holding her tightly a long time.

Well, thought Erica, at least nothing's been said about heads being chopped off.

Presently, Meg stopped sniffling and took a candle from inside the secret door and lit it from another candle burning by the altar. Then she motioned Erica to follow her. They crouched down and shuffled through the open panel. Meg shut it behind them, making use of an obvious handle.

They stood up. In the candlelight there was plenty of headroom. They were in the center of a narrow space. Two more people would make it quite crowded, especially given the size of Meg's enormous skirt. In the back of the room were steep stone steps ascending in a spiral, much like the ones that Erica had descended from the gallery into the chapel.

"Where do those go?" she asked.

"To the turret of the corner chamber, above," said Meg. "There is a secret entryway straight beside the privy."

"And you are going to hide here, until later tonight?" Erica asked.

"Precisely," said Meg. "The Queen shall be staying down the hall—atop the great stairway."

"I know," said Erica.

"Thou knowest?" said Meg. "How wouldst thou?"

"Never mind," said Erica. "And I can make it back here without being seen tonight?"

"With ease," said Meg. "Just make sure thou comest after evening prayers."

"And you will still be here?"

"Why Erica, where think you I would stir in Hengrave, wearing your outlandish garb? For shame, to show my legs thus!"

"These?" said Erica, looking down at her favorite shorts. "These are my baby-blue denims. Don't you make fun of my baby-blue denims, Meg."

"Erica, I would never think to make light of them. I will so much as do you the honor of wearing them, privately, by candlelight, for the length of an afternoon—and evening too." For the first time Meg laughed, a small giggle. Erica thought it sounded so much like the way she herself giggled that she couldn't help giggling too. And then Meg really laughed, her whole skirt shaking. And then Erica. And then they spent so much time shushing each other in case someone should hear that they giggled all over again.

At last they got down to the business of exchanging clothes. In that small space, and with all the many hoops and stays and underthings that Meg had to get out of and Erica had to get into, it was a wonder they accomplished any of it. But before too long, Erica was splendidly dressed and feeling all but suffocated, and Meg was feeling nearly naked, or so she said.

Meg held out the candle and looked Erica up and down. "Thou truly art—mine own self," she said in awe. "Not a soul in Hengrave shall know."

Erica inspected Meg in her baby-blues. "Really, they look great on you," she replied. "Too bad you can't go outside and get yourself a good tan." It was true. Margaret's legs were lily-white from so many years under dresses and stockings and petticoats.

"What meanest thou, a tan?" said Meg.

"Okay, a sunburn," said Erica. "You could settle for that."

Meg wrinkled her nose.

"Now," said Erica, "I suppose I can still make it to Master Edward's chamber?"

"Yes. Do hurry," said Meg.

"Master Edward I think I can handle, if he doesn't ask too many questions. I can just be quiet, pretend I'm nervous about tonight. But what do I do after the lesson? It's not like I'm really you, you know. And I don't quite know my way around yet."

Meg considered, sitting down on the stone step and putting her elbows on her knees. "Stay with my sister Mary," she said. "Go where she goes. Whatever she does, do you also. It is mostly like that anyway—we are together always, unfortunately."

"Unfortunately? How old is she? Will she find me out?"

"If Mary is suspicious of thee, tell her thou wilt wring the neck of her ducky Dickon in the moat. She loves him so that she will obey me in anything to save his life. As for her age, Mary is twelve years this month, more than a summer behind me."

"You're thirteen then?"

Meg nodded.

"Me too," said Erica. Then she paused. She was almost afraid to ask the next obvious question. But she heard herself say, "When is your birthday?"

"The ninth of December," Meg said.

"Funny," said Erica slowly. "That's my birthday."

CHAPTER 9

The Empty Room

WHEN ERICA EMERGED FROM THE chapel into the lower hallway, she half expected to land back in her own time. There would be nuns swooshing about in their purple habits and students slouching by with books. But no such persons seemed to exist—the hallway was full of boys and men, strangely and colorfully clothed in blues and in yellows, walking and running in both directions. She stood in the doorway watching them go back and forth. Calling and shouting echoed from all parts of the house, and a trumpet was sounding just outside the main doors. Whenever one of the boys or men noticed her, he would doff his cap and ever so slightly bend his knee in mid-stride, saying, "G'day, my lady" or "Young Mistress Kytson, good afternoon."

"Good afternoon," she would say in return, even trying to curtsy a bit in her hooped skirt. She found that it collided with the door behind her. She had to stand far into the hallway, where she became an obstacle to all the people rushing by.

"Excuse me," she said, almost knocking one of them down. He was a tall thin boy with a blue wool coat and stockings to match. "What is all this hurry about?"

He looked quite startled to be addressed. "'Tis the Queen, my young lady," he said breathlessly. "She is even earlier than supposed. Her messenger puts her at four mile off, and all is woefully unready. I must now to find fresh rushes for her chamber, and much of the household goes to greet her on the way. You are wanted, I am sure." With that, he hurried off toward the back of the manor house.

This left Erica perplexed. What should she do now? Not stand here and obstruct traffic, certainly. But she could not very well go wandering about the manor without a guide. And she wasn't sure she should go outside—not yet, anyhow. Without being able to think about it very long, she decided to venture at once to the Wilbye Chamber, just as she had at first intended. Perhaps Master Edward and her so-called sister would still be there.

So she walked down the hallway after the boy in the blue coat, swimming both with and against the current of people. They must all be servants, she supposed, dressed in the colors of the household. Soon she came to the great stairs and mounted upward, swinging round the landing with its tall windows that looked out on the west lawn. That was where Katrina and Walter had tumbled with the St. Bernards in the rain-washed evening. How long ago that was, thought Erica—and then she realized it wasn't long ago at all. Precisely the opposite, in fact. This time, the sky still looked sunny enough, but clouds were gathering on the horizon.

At the top of the stairs she stepped past the Queen's chamber and couldn't help peeking in. It was buzzing with servants. They were carrying cloths and furniture, hanging tapestries, making up bedding, airing the room. Something very aromatic was burning in the fireplace. A man bumped into her with an armload of cut green stalks—rushes, she guessed—and dumped them all out on the floor. He looked at her sharply.

"Excuse me," said Erica timidly, and abruptly left, turning down a narrow windowless corridor that led behind the upper part of the great hall. She was tempted to run, but thought better of it when she considered the spectacle she would make in her hooped skirt.

At length the narrow corridor met the top of the smaller stairway she had explored with Pedro. She turned past the head of these stairs, passed by the doors to the linen closet and minstrels gallery, crossed under a small arch into the larger windowed hallway, and came to a halt at the threshold of the familiar room. This time, there was no inscription that read *Wilbye Chamber*. But it was the same doorway.

She knocked quietly.

No one called for her to enter.

She knocked again, and this time put her ear to the door. Hearing nothing, she lifted the latch and pushed inward. The room looked much as it had before, except no one was in it. She stepped inside, moving her feet among the rushes. The early afternoon sky shone against the brilliant blue and yellow curtains, and no fire burned on the hearth. A small table was set up on two trestles next to the virginal, and scattered across it were plates and goblets bearing the remains of someone's noon meal. All of a sudden Erica felt hungry.

She stepped to the trestle table and inspected the leftovers. On a pewter dish were long whitish vegetable stalks half-buried in toasted cheese. She turned up her nose, recognizing this at once—leek casserole. Some things never change. But next to it was some black bread which she found halfway palatable. And one goblet was still full of something that tasted both sweet and bitter— wine, perhaps. She couldn't begin to drink it all, though she felt thirsty enough. It was odd that so much should be left over—almost as if the people who were eating and drinking had left in a hurry before they had finished. Which was likely, she thought. Master Edward and little Mary had probably gone to greet the Queen. And so, probably, should she.

But her attention was now drawn by the fat stringed instrument in the corner—a lute, maybe? The instrument for boys and men that Sister Julian had mentioned? It was strange, the way the top of the neck bent suddenly back, as if it were broken. She stepped closer. The neck was not broken at all. It was simply made that way. She sat down as well as she could in her hooped skirt on one of Master Edward's stools and held the instrument in her lap. The wood was lustrous against her hands, the strings soft. She strummed them once, and they gave a far-off melancholy chord, as pleasing as it was sad. The lute had none of the spirited assurance of the virginal.

She put the instrument down and noticed a row of cases near the wall. Some sprawled open and empty. Others were shut tight. She unlatched the closest one and found another stringed instrument, larger and fatter than the lute. It gave off a rich, deep sound when she plucked its string. There were others like it, and smaller ones like violins. Another row of cases held the wind instruments, none of them remotely like a flute or oboe or clarinet. She tried blowing on a few, but drew no sound but the echo of her own breath. She never had been one for a horn or a harmonica. She hadn't even learned to whistle. Her mouth was made to sing, that was all.

On the other side of the room from all of these instruments, she now took note of a small bed and a chest of drawers. Having already opened up a good many things, she thought she would see what sort of clothes were in the bureau. She had half an idea this was wrong. But she was curious, and carried by the spirit of exploration.

The top drawer contained an array of perfumes and stockings in musky odors and dusky colors. She dabbed her fingers in little bottles, then held up a pair of black hose. They were hardly nylon—more like a thin, worsted cloth. Only a few pair of hose were blue or yellow like those of the servants in the hallways. Maybe the musician was different. She pulled the black pair all the way out of the drawer and let them dangle to her toes. She had to laugh—to think that a grown man could put these on and imagine himself fully dressed.

She was just about to fold up the stockings when she heard the door to the chamber open. Erica gave a start and whirled, her face flushed. *Master Edward*, she wanted to say, *I'm so sorry. I'm so so sorry to be looking through your stockings and things.* But before she could speak at all, she realized the person standing in the door was not Master Edward.

It was Pedro.

He stared at her blankly.

It took Erica more than a moment to recover. But once she did, it was almost a pleasure to see him so confused by the situation.

"Don't just stand in the doorway," she said. "Someone will see you. Come in, come in." She had to walk to the door herself and pull him inside by the hand.

"Erica, what are you wearing?" he said, gawking at her up and down. "What happened to the television? And what are these—" he paused, letting the last word fall like a realization—"instruments."

Erica made no reply. She just stood holding his hand.

"So you weren't lying yesterday." He said it quietly. "You really did find musical instruments here in the chamber."

Erica nodded. She almost smiled.

"I've been reading about them," Pedro went on. It was almost as if he had to talk to regain his poise. "I know what they are now. Yesterday you made me curious, playing that old madrigal, and Sister Julian loaned me a book."

At the mention of Sister Julian, Erica really did smile.

"Here, see?" He dropped her hand. "This is the virginal you were asking about—a double virginal, in fact. In the old parlance, a double pair of virginals. Two keyboards—except they call them rows of jacks—one on top of the other. And these are lutes of all sizes, and viols, and violins—almost like our own. And flutes, and recorders, and sackbuts, and not oboes but *hoboys*. They're old, you know, all from four centuries back."

Then Pedro paused. "But Erica—" He cut himself off and looked at her strangely. "They look so new."

"They *are* new," Erica said quietly.

Now it was Pedro's turn to take her hand and squeeze it tightly. "You don't mean—" he whispered, looking about at the curtains and the empty hearth and the rushes strewn across the floor.

"I do mean," Erica said.

"But how did you get here?"

"Through that door, just like you did, yesterday. This morning I came through the chapel. Apparently there are different ways, if necessary."

"If necessary?"

"I can't really explain it, Pedro. But I think I'm here to help someone—someone named Margaret who looks like me—and who might even be related to me. And maybe to help her whole family. Sister Julian has led me to think so, anyway."

"Sister Julian?" he said. "She's the one who told me to look for you here. No one's been able to find you, Erica. We called for you at lunchtime, but you weren't in your room."

"No," she said. "I most certainly wasn't. It can't be helped. And now they won't find you, either. Pedro, you're going to think this is crazy, but right now I think you had better help yourself to a pair of tights in that bureau over there. You'd better get changed."

"You mean, into doublet and hose?"

"Whatever," said Erica. "Don't worry. I won't look."

Pedro glanced at the chest of drawers uncertainly.

"Do it," ordered Erica.

She stepped to the windows and resolutely looked out to give Pedro time to dress. An old church with a small tower stood just outside. She had seen it already from the dining room below, even in her own time. On the tower was a blue clock, and on the clock was a gold hour hand—that was all. It was after two. Two of the clock. The minutes did not seem to matter.

She stepped closer. The windows were made of diamond panes imbedded in a soft lead lattice. One of them was thrown open. She looked down and saw a narrow moat below—green, brackish, and evil smelling. Like sewage, almost. And for all she knew, it was. But glossy ducks sailed on the surface, and beyond the moat and the small church stretched whitened fields and great green rows of trees. Clouds were moiling across the sky, some of them dark, but the sun still shone, and swallows and sparrows swooped and darted under the eaves and out upon the open land.

England.

She was just about to turn around to see if Pedro had finished dressing when there came a furious knock at the door. Before she could move, it was flung open, and in rushed the tall thin boy in the blue coat—the one she had met in the hallway outside the chapel. He was just as breathless now as then.

"My lady," he said. "Mistress Margaret. Master Edward sends for thee. Thy mother, thy father, thy sister all send for thee. They await the Queen at the edge of the park, just where your father's lands begin. There you are to carry your welcome with the rest, and do thy part. Make haste, make haste. Post haste, they say. You must come anon. A carriage awaits you at the door."

The messenger was in such a hurry that he scarcely noticed Pedro standing by the bureau in blue coat and blue stockings, much like his spindly self. Except Pedro's clothes, being much too large for him, hung awkwardly on every side.

Erica crossed the room to the bureau and fixed the messenger with a frown. "I know it already," she retorted.

"*Betimes,*" whispered Pedro.

"I know it betimes. Master Edward's own servant has come before you to get me—"

"*Prevented you to summon me,*" Pedro whispered.

"—to summon me, and we will come to the carriage at once."

The boy looked Pedro up and down with haughty disdain.

"Leave us," said Erica.

"We will down presently," Pedro told the boy sternly.

Clearly displeased, the messenger left, muttering and biting his lip.

"I guess that fixed him," said Pedro when the door shut.

"Thanks," said Erica. "You really do know the right things to say, don't you?"

"*Cymbeline*," Pedro said. "A very fine production of *Cymbeline*." He puffed on an invisible pipe.

Erica laughed in spite of herself. "You know," she said, "if I weren't so nervous, I could be having some fun."

She smiled at him. "You do look silly, Pedro. Is that the best you could find in those drawers?"

He shrugged and looked down.

"But it can't be helped," she said cheerfully. "We really do have to go." She pulled him by the arm toward the door.

"Who are we meeting?"

"The Queen, like he said. And the whole happy Kytson family, and their chief musician. Plus lots of other people, I'm sure."

"Which queen?" said Pedro.

"Why, Queen Elizabeth, of course."

Pedro stopped. He had a look on his face that meant he was trying to retrieve a forgotten fact. The look disappeared.

"Then it's 1578," he said.

Chapter 10

A Ride in the Country

ONCE OUT OF THE CHAMBER, PEDRO and Erica hurried down the back stairs and through the crowded hallways to the main entrance of Hengrave. Outside the great double doors, which now stood wide open, they crossed a stone bridge over the putrid moat. At the end of the bridge a small black carriage was waiting, its large red wheels thick and clumsy. A driver wearing a dusty cap sat holding the reins of a pair of ponies. Behind him was an open bench that would fit two. When he saw Erica he leapt from his perch, doffed his cap, and handed her up into the carriage. Pedro climbed up after her, or tried to, but the driver turned and cuffed him away with the back of his hand.

"Who d' ye think ye be," he snarled, "makin' as if t' ride with thy betters?"

Pedro staggered backward. The blow had landed right on his nose. He touched it as if checking to see if it were broken.

"He is needed," said Erica sternly. "By the chief musician."

"Aye, as like as not," grumbled the surly driver. "And Spanish vermin to boot." He turned his back and Erica put out her hand for Pedro, who mounted very cautiously.

"Are you okay?" she whispered. She didn't know which was worse for him—getting whacked on the nose or being called "Spanish vermin."

Pedro nodded yes, he was fine, but she could tell he was shaken. The driver was a short, thick man with knobby warts across his face. He now picked up a long black whip and cracked it over the backs of the ponies. Pedro flinched. But Erica was not afraid, for she was beginning to understand some of the power that she had. All sorts of people had to do whatever she said because she was the elder daughter of the house. She thought it must feel something like this to be the Queen.

As the carriage lurched forward she saw they were in a graveled courtyard, surrounded by rows of stables and workshops, none of which she remembered from their arrival at Hengrave on the coach. She caught glimpses of men who were forking hay, shoveling stalls, and carting loads of trunks and tables, each calling out to his neighbor. Hounds and spaniels ran back and forth, barking, and bells rang wildly in the steeple of the church next door. And now she too, bouncing along, was part of the hurry.

The carriage drove straight on through the courtyard and out through an arch in a wall between two buildings. They crossed another stone bridge over a moat and then they were in open country. Whitened fields fell away on either hand. The driver cracked his whip over the heads of the ponies and sent them trotting quickly down a lane bordered with deep ditches and triple columns of young trees, newly planted. They might have been elms. The lane continued before them in a straight line to a wood in the distance. Erica felt the wind in her face and turned and saw the towers of Hengrave over the tops of the out-buildings. How grand and curious they looked, rising and receding at the end of the driveway under the clouds.

She gave Pedro a nudge and he smiled thinly. His nose seemed a little bloody. "Are you sure you're okay?" she said.

He sniffed and nodded. It appeared as if he were going to cry, so Erica took his hand in hers. She had half an idea the driver shouldn't see this.

At length the road left the saplings behind and became quite bumpy. In the back of the carriage the two of them began to bang up and down on the hard bench. It reminded Erica of playing on the teeter-totter with some-one who jumps off the other end and leaves you to come crashing down. At first it is fun, but then it hurts.

"Excuse me," she called to the driver, letting go Pedro's hand. "Could you slow up a bit? It's rough back here."

"I must post haste," he called back impatiently. "Thy father's orders."

Erica sighed and looked at Pedro. His nose was really bleeding now. She searched all about her skirt and finally found a handkerchief hidden in a small pocket. It was made of lace. "Here," she said, and wiped his nose and told him to pinch it. She had him hold the handkerchief tightly against his nostrils. If only they would get there. She wanted to ask the driver how much farther it was. But perhaps this was something the real Meg would already know. She kept quiet.

After much jolting and bouncing down the road, Erica saw a double line of carts and wagons heading directly for them. They made a white cloud of dust on just this side of the wood, which was now nearby. Before their carriage reached the wood, they encountered the first of these carts and wagons, which came on two abreast, piled high with trunks and provisions. There was no room for the carriage to drive around them—they took up the entire road, and then some, kicking up dust as far in the distance as Erica could see.

Their driver stopped the carriage and cursed. "Make way," he cried, "for the young Mistress Kytson."

The driver of the cart directly in front of them stopped his horses. "Make way yourself," he shouted back, "for the baggage train of her majesty the Queen! Off the road, you son of a beggar, or I'll be mending potholes with your pretty ponies!"

Then he cracked his whip, and the cart and horses went forward again at a smart pace as if their carriage were not there. Erica's driver lashed his whip too, trying to whirl them out of the way. The ponies reared and whinnied, then shot to the side, and the carriage lurched into the ditch. There it listed cockeyed, half on its side and one red wheel spinning in air. Pedro and Erica found themselves tangled together, hanging on as if they were about to ride a sinking ship into the sea.

As the carts and wagons drove by, the men jeered. "Lost your way?" said one. "The bloody road's over 'ere." Their driver shook his fist at them, but they only laughed.

Finally he turned and told Erica to get out of the carriage as best she could. Fortunately she and Pedro were tilted close to the field on the far side of the ditch. It was just a hop.

"You see the wood yonder?" said the driver, pointing just ahead of them. "There it is thy family and the chief musician await thee. Taste thy legs. Quickly now. And never tell thy father that I did not bring thee as far and as hastily as I might."

"We thank you," said Erica prettily. Not knowing what else to do, she curtsied to the driver from the edge of the field.

In holding out the edges of her white, hooped skirt, however, she found one side of it torn and smudged from their upheaval in the carriage. The other side was smeared with bright blood from Pedro's handkerchief, of which he had lost hold.

"Oh dear," she said. "Oh dear, oh dear. This won't do at all."

"What?" said Pedro. Then he saw. "Oh, Erica—I'm so sorry. Really, I am."

He checked his nose. "I think it has stopped bleeding," he said. "I promise I won't do anything else to your new dress."

This was little consolation. But there was nothing to be done. Even as they stood by the roadside, a thick fog of dust from the many wagons passing by was settling on their clothing. What white was left in her sorry skirt was quickly turning a dull brown.

"We'd better go," she said coldly. It clearly wasn't Pedro's fault but she felt like blaming somebody, and he was conveniently at hand. As they made their way through the fields alongside the road, she made a point of not speaking a word to him. The wagons went past by the score, and it seemed like every one of the drivers had a rude word for the bloody and bedraggled pair. But Erica said nothing to the wagon drivers either.

By the time they reached the wood, the army of wagons had all passed. Behind them came a multitude of men on horseback, all wearing bright red coats with the letters *ER* displayed in gold. A smart banner bore the same golden initials. "Elizabeth Regina," Pedro whispered to her, apparently thinking to break their silence with a useful piece of information. "It means Elizabeth the Queen. These are her serving-men, all wearing the Queen's uniform—her livery—to show that they belong to her."

But Erica wasn't listening. As they began to skirt the edge of the wood, tiptoeing between the horsemen and the trees, she thought she saw someone ahead who was frantically waving and calling to her. A few paces further and she saw that it was Master Edward, wearing his new dark doublet and hose. She ran to greet him, leaving Pedro to fend for himself.

Roses Are Red

"MARGARET!" CRIED THE MUSIC master. "Where hast thou been? The Queen's own person is nearly upon us, and you must do your part with the rest."

"My part?" she said uncertainly.

He looked at her dress and frowned.

"Thy part," he said—"to show thyself as a fairy princess with thy sister, and after saying thy pretty piece which thou hast conned, to present unto her majesty the rich jewel which thy father holds for thee in waiting. But come, now, into the wood to hide until the Queen appear."

She followed him behind the trees, wishing she had Pedro with her to interpret. What did Master Edward mean about her saying a pretty piece which she had conned? *Conned*? Was she supposed to have memorized something—a poem or a speech? How would she be able to say anything unless she had Pedro to help her? She looked back and saw him standing uncertainly at the edge of the road.

"*Psst!*" she called, waving him toward her.

He smiled and followed. Erica felt a little relieved.

But only a little. Master Edward stopped behind a large oak, and there waited a company of people she was sure she was supposed to know. Beside a number of servants and musicians holding flutes and drums was a little girl, strawberry blonde, dressed in white. She stood nervously on one foot and then the other, picking the bark off of the tree. There was a sharp-faced woman in rich blue velvet, intently plucking at her sleeve. And there was a very stout and handsome man, standing with his arms folded and legs spread apart. Around his neck was a gold chain.

"Why Meg, Meg," the man said in a hearty voice. "I told them you would not fail to come. Thou wouldst not disappoint thy father." He unfolded his arms and gave her a tremendous hug.

"What hast thou done to thy dress?" said the sharp-faced woman she took to be Meg's mother. "Thou hast besmirched it woefully!"

Erica felt the color rise in her face. "The carriage," she stammered. "It tipped over. It tippeth over—however you say it." This last she added under her breath.

"The driver shall be whipped!" said the man.

"Oh no," said Erica. "It wasn't his fault. You see, the wagons—"

"There's no time, Meg," the small girl interrupted. She was almost squeaking, her voice was so high. "We needs must don the rest of our attire and say over our parts. The Queen approacheth."

"What is't o'clock?" her father asked peremptorily.

"I think it be near four of the clock," said Master Edward. "Though one cannot tell. There is no clock in the forest."

"Who knows not that?" said Mistress Kytson, glaring at him. "Don't play such a fool."

"Make yourselves ready all," said her husband. "Meg, take this jewel and keep it well between thy hands. You know the proper moment to present it to her majesty." With that he pressed a gleaming emerald into her palm. It was cut and beveled to a perfect square. "Ah, my Meg. I know thou wilt not disappoint me."

As he released her from another embrace her supposed mother took her aside. "Look you that you say thy piece promptly and with good wit," she whispered sharply. "Thou knowest thy father has high hopes to be made a knight of the realm. 'Twill be a credit to all our family. Far better than to be imprisoned like poor Master Rokewood, and Hengrave forfeit to the crown like Euston Hall. Think on it, and let thyself for once in thy life be plainly attentive to our welfare." She gave Erica a long hard look, and then passed her on to Master Edward.

He put some kind of gauzy stuff into her hair, draped her with pearls, and fitted her face with a silver mask. In one hand he placed a thin silver wand. In the other she held the square-cut emerald. Apparently she was now ready.

"Mary," she whispered, hoping she had the right name. The strawberry blonde girl was attired much like herself, except that her mask and wand were golden. "Do you speak first, or is it me?"

Mary looked at her in alarm. "Why, I do speak first, after Father. Knowest not that? Thou art the very last."

"Just checking," said Erica. She looked over at Pedro, who was standing with a knot of servants. He saw her and shrugged. There was not much he could do.

Just then a messenger burst through the trees. "The serving-men and the escort from Suffolk have now passed," he called out. "The French ambassadors approach, and the Queen and her councilors come immediately behind."

At this news, everyone rushed toward the road. Master Edward made the girls stand behind a screen of bushes. He and the other musicians took up stations behind them, flutes at ready. The others stood at the roadside, Thomas Kytson at their head, his legs spread wide. Through the bushes Erica could make out horses. They were sleek and richly caparisoned with blue cloths covered with emblems that looked like lilies. Riding them were men wearing pointed beards and huge hats of all colors. Feathery plumes waved in the wind or sagged in the dust. The men were laughing, and speaking loudly to each other in words that sounded strange and oily. French, she supposed.

But they were soon past. Behind them a team of four horses pulled an elaborate gilt carriage, much larger than the one in which Pedro and Erica had ridden. Trumpeters rode on either side, and behind them were grave English men on horseback. Erica stood on tiptoe to try to see who was in the carriage. Mary pinched her. "Down, wanton," she whispered fiercely. "We are not to be seen."

The carriage came to a stop before them, and the trumpets blew. "Kneel before the Queen of England!" a herald cried.

All at the roadside kneeled—and not just on one knee, but on both, as if in prayer.

"Does that mean us too?" Erica asked.

"Hush," said Mary.

"God save your grace," called Meg's father.

The others echoed, "God save your grace."

"God save you all, my loyal subjects," came a high, piping voice from the carriage. "Please rise."

Everyone at the roadside stood up again, their caps in their hands.

Try as she might, Erica could not see the Queen. The thickest part of the screen of bushes grew in her way. But she dared not move.

Then she saw Master Kytson step into the road before the carriage and make an elaborate bow. "Insofar as our means be able," he said in a loud voice, "we give your majesty great welcome, more to be valued by our rich intent than by what little we can perform. Hengrave Hall is deeply honored by your presence, and all that we have under roof or bough is dedicated to thy good pleasure and thy good comfort."

He went on to say more—things about her illustrious graces, her generous bounty, her boundless virtues, her wisdom beyond earthly measure—until Erica thought he would never stop. She had an idea he didn't mean the half of it, and wondered if the Queen thought the same.

But Erica was not listening very hard for the simple reason that she was worried about what she herself would say when it came her turn. She was supposed to give the Queen the jewel in her hand—this much was clear. But what before that?

Suddenly she became aware of Pedro nudging her at one side. "Do you know what you're going to do?" he asked, whispering.

"I have no idea," she hissed.

"Quiet," said Mary, glaring at her through her golden mask. "Thou wilt give us away before our time."

"Quiet yourself," said Erica rudely. She didn't have to answer to a little sister, hers or not.

"I've been thinking," Pedro said quietly. "I've heard my mother explain about this sort of occasion. Usually, when people who are dressed up like fairies or like goddesses jump out of the bushes to greet the Queen they have some kind of argument about who likes her best, that sort of thing."

"An argument?" Erica said. "I can do that."

"When hast thou been so familiar with serving-men?" Mary hissed. "Meg, for shame. Keep silent, I say."

"And I say, I'll talk if I want, if you want to see your little ducky Dickon alive again. I'll wring his neck, little Mistress Mary, if you don't keep your nose out of my affairs."

Mary huffed.

Erica smiled proudly, pleased to have remembered Meg's advice. "See?" said Erica to Pedro. "I can have an argument whenever I want."

Pedro still looked concerned. "I'll stay close," he said. "I'll help if I can."

He moved away, and at that moment Master Kytson finished his speech. The voice from the carriage now said, "We thank thee for thy welcome and this promise of thy gracious hospitality."

Master Kytson made another low bow and then nodded to the musicians who were hiding behind the girls in the bushes. At once they began to play their flutes in a high piercing melody. Drums began to beat quickly. It made Erica wish she could dance. She had never been much of a dancer.

Mary grasped her arm. "'Tis our sign, Meg. Up now."

Erica let Mary lead her into the road beside the carriage. They stood together in a little space in front of the household. A murmur ran through the grave men who flanked the carriage on horseback. Erica heard one of them say, "What pretty poppets these be." The French ambassadors, however, turned up their noses and yawned.

But what Erica saw most of all was Queen Elizabeth herself. She sat high up in the carriage, alone, in a silver gown. Her collar stood out on every side and jewels and pearls hung from her neck. Her face was very white and pinched, and her hair a strawy red color. As for her eyes, Erica had never felt a gaze so severe and knowing.

Erica must have been staring dumbly, for Mary nudged her hard and said, "Dance, Meg. We are to begin."

Erica was mortified. Though she would have liked to dance, in truth she was no better at it than blowing on a fife or flute. She watched Mary swing her golden wand through the air and twirl about, and tried to do something similar. If she were supposed to be in synchrony with her sister she was much a failure, for Erica was always one or two steps behind at best. Sometimes Mary would shuffle and clog her feet in such an intricate way that Erica simply stood and watched, waving her little silver wand as if that were all she was supposed to do.

Finally the music stopped. Without warning, Mary turned to Erica and threw down her wand. Was she really angry, Erica wondered, or was this part of the plan?

"For shame, for shame," Mary said in her squeaky voice, "that thou shouldst show thy wicked self before this Queen. Thou of the night, I of the day we fairies be. Our gracious sovereign is eternal sunrise in yon heaven's eye, and ruleth like the chariot of Phaeton. 'Tis only meet that I and my diurnal race should greet her in these happy realms of Hengrave's wood. Thou and thy kind must slink away with wolves and shadows of the fen, and never think to bring thy dark before this Queen."

Then Mary stopped speaking. Erica was quite sure it was her turn. There was only one problem: she hadn't understood much of anything Mary had said. But gestures she did understand. So she threw her silver wand to the ground, just as Mary had thrown down her golden one. Then she stepped forward dramatically, and opened her mouth.

Nothing came out.

She could feel the Queen gazing at her coolly, inspecting her torn and bloody gown.

And nothing came out of her mouth.

One of the French ambassadors began to laugh.

She felt herself turning red. Her heart was pounding.

She looked for Pedro. He was standing as close as he dared, and she heard him whisper, "*The moon.* Say the Queen is like the goddess of *the moon.*"

And then, to her wonder, the Queen addressed her. "I hope I have not put thee out of thy part. Prithee, say on. Be not afraid." Her voice was tart but there seemed to be the slightest twinkle in her eye.

So Erica took courage and spoke. "I wonder at thy argument, young golden fairy," she heard herself saying to Mary. "Is not the Queen as much the Queen of night as day? Is she not like the moon in her—in her—in her—" And here she began to falter like a broken record. She had no idea what would make the Queen in the carriage like the moon.

"*Is she not like the virgin huntress sweeping o'er the shades of night?*" Pedro whispered frantically.

"Is she not like the virgin huntress pulling down the nightshades?" Erica said. "I mean, sweeping the kitchen in the night? I mean—oh dear."

"*Is she not like—*" Pedro began, but then he was roughly jerked away by Master Edward, who had put down his flute and come to investigate at close hand. Erica saw a terrible frown of displeasure on the musician's face.

She looked at Mary, hoping she had said enough, that her turn was over, but Mary looked back at her wide-eyed and apparently speechless. She looked at her supposed father and saw a look of grim helplessness in his eyes.

She looked at her supposed mother and saw that she was seething with anger, mutilating the threads in her sleeve.

Then, suddenly, Erica rushed to the side of the carriage and held out the emerald in her hand. She made a little bow and said, "Roses are red, violets are blue, this is a jewel and it's for you." Then she held it up, and the Queen reached down and accepted the emerald with a nod.

There was a slight patter of applause from the Queen's men as she held the emerald up to the light. Then she fixed Erica with her knowing eyes. It seemed she was going to denounce her as a proven imposter. Then she would say, *Off with her head*!

But instead she heard the Queen say, "I thank both you and yours for this rare stone. And as for your speech, young fairy of the night, it is the best that ever I heard. You shall have my hand."

Everyone kneeled as the Queen extended her hand again. Erica held it very briefly, then dropped to her knees like all the others. She could not bear to look up.

Then she heard the slap of reins, and the carriage was gone.

CHAPTER 12

A Little Push

ERICA FELT GENTLE HANDS PULLING her up. It was Master Edward. She let him guide her back to the edge of the road. "We must give way," he said, "for the Queen's councilors." He sounded tired.

She looked and saw the men in black go riding after the gilt carriage. They all seemed grim and determined, not at all as if they were on a holiday. It occurred to Erica that it might be a little exhausting to follow the Queen all about the countryside for weeks on end.

Behind them came an irregular group of well-dressed women, some on horseback and others seated in carriages. The dust had spoiled their gowns as well. Some of them were waving fans to ward off the sultry air and looking up anxiously. The sky was now dark with clouds.

"Who are these?" asked Erica innocently.

"Ladies-in-waiting," said Master Edward. "And certain noblewomen of the realm."

Just then a particularly splendid coach rolled by, almost as ornate as the Queen's. An old woman with a hard, shrewd face looked down from the coach at Erica. She narrowed her eyes as if studying her for a special purpose.

"And who is that?" Erica whispered to Master Edward.

"The Countess of Shrewsbury," he said. "Better known as Bess of Hardwick. The richest woman in the kingdom. And like to be richer, the way she schemes. All praise her, but none trust her."

Just as the Countess of Shrewsbury passed, a burst of thunder echoed in the distance, and raindrops began to pelt the dust in the road. Several of the women screamed and put their fans over their heads. Others laughed. Everyone urged their horses on. The last of the noble-women and ladies-in-waiting passed by, and the road was empty except for the Kytsons and their servants. Erica felt as if all eyes were upon her.

"What hast thou done?" screeched Mistress Kytson. Her voice came slicing through the air like the raindrops that were starting to fall. "Dost thou mean to make us all a laughingstock?"

"Now, now, my dear," said her husband uneasily. "The Queen pronounced herself quite pleased. We all heard it."

"The Queen!" said Mistress Kytson. "The Queen was mocked, and only mocked us in return."

To this her husband gnawed his lip without replying. Erica could tell his hopes were half-hearted.

"Well, bring the carriage round," he burst out finally. "Let's not just stand here in the rain." Several servants went running off into the wood to obey his order.

"We'll all to Hengrave to feast the Queen as we can, and pleasure her with music after." At the mention of the word *music*, Erica thought he gave her a pleading look.

Thunder crashed once again, this time closer. The rain began to beat down in earnest.

"It was the strange servant boy," Mary piped up in her squeaky voice.

Her father was only half listening. He was holding out his hands in the rain, palms upward, shaking his head.

"'Twas the servant boy that distracted her," Mary went on. "She always beforehand knew her lines. I know not why she hath been so familiar with him."

"'Tis true," said Master Edward. "I caught him myself whispering at her whilst she was speaking her part to the Queen."

"We'll have him whipped," proclaimed Mistress Kytson. "Who knows the stripling? Where makes he? He will be no more conversant with our daughters."

She looked about imperiously while horses and carriages belonging to the household began to be led out of the wood. No one seemed to know this serving-boy, or where he had gone. In the excitement Master Edward had loosed his hold after pulling Pedro away from the fairies. Now he was not to be seen. In any case, everyone was more interested in getting back to Hengrave than in searching for the strange boy.

Erica was worried for him, but she was far too miserable to keep her thoughts entirely on Pedro. She was handed into a covered carriage with Mary by the music master. As they waited for the carriage to start, he stood in the rain and looked up at them mournfully.

"Tonight, my little pupils," he said. "Tonight you play as never before. Promise me."

"I'll try," said Erica weakly.

Mary sniffed, and said nothing.

It was a long ride back. The dust rapidly turned to mud and stuck to the carriage wheels like gum. The rain drummed on the taut leather roof of the carriage, which eventually began to leak, dripping water down the back of Erica's neck. Mary would not talk at all, which was just as well, for Erica had no desire to speak with her. Her willingness to betray Pedro—to a whipping, no less—made her an object of loathing. It hardly occurred to Erica that Mary was only acting out of embarrassment and disappointment—and in any case could hardly be expected to know who Pedro was. No, she could only think that Mary had accused Pedro out of little-sisterly spite. What mattered now was to get her back.

As she meditated her revenge, Erica noticed a horseman who had drifted back from the procession, loitering at the side of the road. When the elder Kytsons passed by, he nodded politely, and then he ambled up alongside Erica's carriage. He was a young man, dressed in a fine white velvet coat all ruined by the mud and wet. The rain poured off his wide-brimmed hat, and several feathers lay soaked atop it in disarray.

"The young ladies Kytson, I presume?" the young man said. He smiled hard—a little too hard—as if something were making him nervous.

Erica looked at him curiously. He had blonde hair and fine features. "You presume right," she said flippantly.

He swept off his hat in the rain and made a little bow from his horse. "So very pleased," he said. He looked at Erica in particular. "So very, very pleased," he said, as if he had run out of any other words to say.

What a strange man. He had to be almost twice her age, yet acted like a shy boy in the seventh grade. "So what's your name?" she said. "Or thy name—whatever."

The man looked taken aback, as if he were not prepared to impart this information. At that moment a crack of thunder split the air right over their heads. There were shouts and screams.

"I must go," said the man. "Someone may need assistance." And with that he rode off, spattering mud from his horse's hooves into the carriage. Erica saw him go at a gallop all the way to Hengrave, which was now approaching through the rain.

It's you that needs assistance, she thought, shaking her head. She turned to Mary. "And who might that be?"

Mary shrugged her damp shoulders and tossed her head. "I know not," she said. "Some man. Some fine young knight or gentleman who no doubt wishes to marry thee."

"Me?" said Erica, thrown into a genuine panic. "Marry me? I'm thirteen years old!"

"So be many," Mary said.

Erica was left to ponder what that meant. She had to be kidding.

"Maybe he wants to marry you," Erica said. "How do you know?"

"Thou art the heir," Mary said. "Because our brother died at birth, who marries you, marries Hengrave. You know this well already, surely."

"But you're prettier," Erica said sarcastically. "I saw him looking at you, Mary."

She tossed her head, unwilling to be shaken. "I should not blame him," she said. "She who forgets her part before the Queen is like to forget her vows before a husband. Thou art naught, sister. Thou art very naught."

"Thou art ugly, sister. Thou art very ugly," Erica retorted.

Mary stuck out her tongue. "Foul is fair. And if not, I care not. If to be beautiful were to be favored as you, 'tis better to be ugly then."

It made Erica dislike her all the more.

Soon their carriage pulled through the low arch and into the outer courtyard. The area by this time was a welter of wagons and confusion. Ladies were being handed out of carriages, horses led to the stables, and luggage hauled across the moat into the main entrance of Hengrave Hall. Apparently the Queen had already gone inside. Their driver, a slow patient man this time, maneuvered the carriage as close to the entrance as he could. Master Edward appeared from nowhere to help them out onto the gravel. His fine new clothes were smeared with mud and sagged and clung in just the places they had puffed out fashionably. Erica felt sorry for him.

Once out in the rain themselves, she and Mary hurried to the stone bridge over the moat. They were halfway across it when Mary stopped and leaned over the low stone wall on one side. "Dickon!" she cried. "I have come to see thee. I have no bread to give thee now, but I shall anon."

Erica heard a loud quacking. She looked past Mary's shoulder and saw a row of ducks below, swimming out from under the bridge to where the raindrops dappled the water.

"Dickon!" squeaked Mary in her irritating little way. She was leaning far over the wall and waving to her favorite duck. "Dost thou know the Queen is here? Thou must swim and quack. Thou must say thy part. Thou must not forget it like my sister."

When she heard that, something in Erica gave way. She took a short fierce step toward Mary in just the way she would menace Walter whenever he stood and taunted her in the door to her room. But on the rough wet cobblestones, she slipped. It was only a little slip. But as she quickly regained her balance, she gave Mary the slightest shove with the turn of her hip. It was enough. With an awful shriek the girl tumbled over the wall and landed headfirst in the water. There was a resounding splash, and ducks flew in all directions. A rough laughter spread across the courtyard.

"Master Edward!" Erica shouted. "Mary has fallen into the moat!"

She looked over the wall and saw her come to the surface, flailing and gasping. Her skirt was spread like a white lily pad all around her.

Master Edward took one glimpse and went sailing over the low wall in a single leap. He landed just next to Mary, went under, came up gulping for air, and put his arm around the girl. It soon became apparent, however, that neither of them knew how to swim. Mary clung to the music master for dear life, and the result was that both of them sank again beneath the water. There were bubbles, there were wellings from the slimy deep, and then they both appeared once more, each looking more panicked than ever.

"What have I done?" Erica whispered to herself. "Oh what have I what have I what have I done?"

It was all happening so quickly, and yet so slowly, and no one was doing anything. In fact, some people were still laughing. Erica was ready to leap the wall herself when a tall thin boy—she recognized him at once as the one she had twice met inside the hall—grabbed a shovel from a wagon, ran to the moat, and reached it out handle-first to the drowning pair. They were about to go down a third time when Master Edward grabbed the shaft. The boy pulled. Mary and the music master went partly underwater again, but they hung on, and the tall thin boy brought them to the edge of the moat. By this time, others saw the seriousness of the situation and crowded round to lend a hand. Soon they had dragged the man and girl up onto the wet gravel, where they both lay choking and spitting in the rain. Their clothes were covered with weeds and sludge.

Erica stood trembling on the stone bridge, greatly appalled at what she had done. She had just slipped in the rain, she repeated to herself. Lost her footing and bumped into her little sister the way you might bump into an elderly woman in the aisle of a moving train.

Mary's parents were summoned from inside the manor. Mistress Kytson rushed to her side and knelt whimpering over her younger daughter. "Of all the days thou couldst have chosen to fall into the moat," she scolded.

Mary coughed feebly and lay quite limp. It seemed she wanted to say something but was unable. The music master was not in much better condition.

"How art thou, man?" said Master Kytson, standing with his legs spread. "Hast saved my daughter? An it be so, thou shalt be rewarded, surely."

Soon servants appeared and wrapped the half-drowned pair in blankets and carried them into the hall to be cared for. As Mary was borne across the bridge, Erica tried to catch her eye. She looked back in a listless way. Erica was not sure if Mary even saw her.

Mary's parents followed after. "But the music," muttered Mistress Kytson on the bridge. "What of that? Who shall play the virginals with Meg, here?"

"Fie, lady. A little water, a little water," said her husband. "The both of them shall be fit as monkeys by banquet time."

But Erica had a funny feeling that Meg's father was very wrong.

CHAPTER 13

Eavesdropping

I^F HENGRAVE HALL HAD BEEN CROWDED before, it was even more tumultuous now that the Queen and her train had arrived. Rain-soaked guests were being directed to their chambers, and dozens of trunks carried through the halls in their wake. Erica stood inside the entrance out of the rain and wondered where she should go. To her chamber, probably, like all the rest, so that she could change out of her wet clothes. But she had no idea which room was hers. And unfortunately, this was just the sort of thing she could not ask.

Part of her wanted to slip away into the chapel and find Meg. She could get her own clothes again and then simply walk through a door back to her own time and family. At least she hoped that were possible—she realized she had not allowed herself to think otherwise. But something told her it was not the proper hour. She had promised Meg that she would play the virginal before the Queen. Though everything else had gone wrong, she would keep that promise. She truly would.

It pleased her to feel this renewed resolve, and gave her the courage to wander into the manor house in hopes of finding her own chamber and clean, dry clothes. First she meandered back toward the kitchen, where wonderful smells of savory sauces and roasting meat made her mouth begin to water. But this did not seem the right place. Then she climbed the small stairs in back of Master Edward's chamber. She went to his door and heard him coughing and sneezing inside. No, she would not go in there.

So she turned back to the top of the stairs and went down the narrow hallway toward the Queen's appointed chamber. Men with swords slouched against the walls of the hallway as if they had nowhere to go. They eyed her derisively, touching their caps. She could hardly stand the feeling that they were staring at her after she had passed by.

There were many rooms off the outside of this corridor, and most of them seemed to be occupied. But when Erica was almost to the Queen's chamber she found a door left open upon an empty room. It was quite small, but seemed to be lavishly furnished. The guard beside the open door arched his eyebrows at her and sneered. What was it that made these people so entirely disagreeable? She decided she had had enough. Without taking too much thought, she flung herself into the chamber and slammed the door behind her.

There, she thought. If she were not in her own room, at least she had a place in which to gather her wits away from those awful men in the hallway. She looked about to take in her new surroundings. There was no bed—just two red velvet chairs with footstools, and a chessboard on a low round table between them. A window at the end of the room showed that the rain had ceased. She walked around the chairs and looked out. There below her the sun was shining under the clouds on a small city of white tents erected in a pasture. She supposed these were for servants and people of lesser rank. They couldn't all fit in the manor house. She found herself wondering if the horseman who had stopped by their carriage were staying inside or out.

When she turned from the window, it struck her that the most remarkable parts of the room were two thick tapestries, one on the wall to her left and one on the wall to her right. They hung like rugs from floor to ceiling. They reminded her of the painted scene on the virginal in the musician's chamber. One was of a tree in a garden loaded down with golden apples. The apples seemed to be woven from thread that really was gold. A dragon slept under the tree, and three very beautiful girls danced in a circle next to the dragon. Outside the garden, over a wall, a strong, hairy man with a club was peering in. Would he fight the dragon, or steal the apples, or fall in love with one of the girls?

The tapestry across the room also featured golden apples. A man and a woman were running a race, and the man had dropped a golden apple. The woman seemed to be pausing to inspect it. She'll lose the race that way, Erica thought. Off to the side, a handsome young man with golden curls was pondering three other women, chin in hand, and they in turn were fighting over yet another golden apple. The three women were wearing loose robes and sheets that did not stay on well. Perhaps they were goddesses. The young man was trying to decide which one deserved the apple, or who was the most beautiful, or which he would choose for himself. It was curious, the way the two tapestries repeated themselves and yet told different stories. Erica was sure she liked the young man with the golden curls better than the one in the race or the hairy one with the menacing club. She hoped he would make the right choice, whatever it was.

And he seemed so real. Erica put out her hand to touch him. She found to her surprise that the tapestry moved backward at the brush of her hand. She pushed it farther. For some reason, there was considerable space between the hanging and the wall. Perhaps the woven material stayed fresher and drier that way. She stepped to the end of it near the window and pulled back on the edge. There was almost room for a person to stand.

At just that moment she heard a noise. The latch was lifting on the door. Erica let go of the hanging and stood upright with a jolt. Who could it be? And how could she justify being here? Trembling all over, she watched the door open inward. And before it could open all the way, she found herself pulling back the hanging again and scrambling behind it. She was right—there was just enough room for her. But her stiff hooped skirt—that was a problem. She crushed it against the front of her legs as well as she could, but Erica was sure that the tapestry was bulging out even so. It was like playing hide and seek as a young child and trying to stand behind the drapes in the living room. She had never managed that trick without giving herself away. But it was too late to change positions. She heard a pair of footsteps enter, and then another. The door closed.

There was much rustling of gowns on the floor. The two visitors must be women, Erica thought. She held her breath in the strange silence. One of the persons sat down on the velvet chair just in front of Erica. The other remained standing, and broke the silence in a low but insistent voice.

"Your majesty, if you will vouchsafe me a word. To be brief with thee, it is more meet that Hengrave should come to my heirs than be made forfeit to the crown."

"Go up!" said the one in the chair. "Thou art bold and saucy. But your reason, Bess. Give me thy reason."

Erica gulped. This was the Queen speaking, less than five feet away from her on the other side of the tapestry. The other sounded considerably older. Bess, she thought. Bess. Bess. Then she remembered the flinty woman who had looked at her from the ornate coach. Bess of Hardwick, the musician had said, Countess of Shrewsbury. The richest woman in the kingdom.

"My reason," said the Countess, "is as much or more to your advantage as to mine. There is no talk in all of Suffolk these two days but that of the imprisonment of young Master Rokewood and thy seizure of Euston Hall. I make no scruple against it. Your majesty must put down all popish plots and Romish traitors. Yet I would advise thee to be sparing in these punishments. Rokewood and Euston Hall are sufficient to inspire fear and obedience in thy loyal subjects. Add Thomas Kytson and Hengrave to thy displeasure, however, and thou art like to inspire rebellion."

"Yet Master Kytson is the staunchest Catholic of them all," said the Queen. "I have his letter pledging his soul to the contrary, but I do never believe it. His mother harbored my sister Mary in these walls in the days of my lamented cousin, Lady Jane Grey. And I doubt not he has several priests in hiding now."

"Catholic he may be," said the Countess. "Faithful to Rome he may be. But Thomas Kytson is no traitor, nor never like to become one. Dine with him, smile upon him, give him a knighthood if thou wilt—but do not cast him into prison and take away his house and his lands."

"From thy heirs?" asked the Queen coyly.

"Yes," said the Countess. "From my youngest, Charles Cavendish, and his issue. He did make good view of her, as did I, after she so clumsily gave to your majesty some slight jewel. I think her plain and homely enough, but my dear son is easily pleased. He was so complacent as to declare himself capable of loving the creature."

The Countess gave a cruel little laugh, and Erica felt her stomach swim. Mary had been exactly right. The young man on horseback really did want to marry her. At least his mother wanted him to. She didn't like the mother at all, whatever she thought of Charles Cavendish.

"Speak not so harshly, Bess," said the Queen. "Better persons than young Meg Kytson have lost their tongue in our royal presence. 'Tis a sign of reverence and respect, and more than anything minds me of the loyalty of this household."

At this, Erica smiled behind the tapestry. She felt warm all over.

"You give your permission then—your permission for the match?" said the Countess.

"I give nothing until my stomach be full after the most weary travel of this day. The ale in Suffolk is not so near as light and tart as I should wish. If just one of these houses should serve good ale—'twould save scores of Catholic gentlemen from years of confinement in the Tower."

"Your grace—" the Countess began.

"I shall think on't, Bess!" the Queen snapped. "I shall think on't. You shall know soon enough. I trust this audience is ended?"

"Yes, your majesty." The Countess sounded almost sarcastic. Erica wondered that she would treat the Queen so rudely.

She heard Queen Elizabeth rise from her chair and step firmly to the door. It quickly opened, and Bess of Hardwick followed her out of the room. For a moment the door was left ajar. Then someone closed it again. The room was empty. Erica stood quietly for a few more minutes to make sure. Then she came out from behind the hanging, gasping hard. It was as if she had run a footrace all the time she had been hiding.

The light in the window was lower and later. Erica looked out and saw dozens and dozens of courtiers and serving-men milling about the white tents. She was grateful to be standing alone in the room again, and more than amazed by what she had heard.

But what was this?

Just under the window a blonde young man with fine features was looking up and waving a glove. To her, it seemed. He wore a cautious smile on his face. How odd. It was the son of the Countess. Charles. Yes, Charles Cavendish.

She blushed and smiled, then turned away into the room.

CHAPTER 14

Sisters Again

WHEN ERICA OPENED THE DOOR back into the corridor, she was deathly afraid the men-at-arms would ask her what she was doing there and haul her before the Queen. But the one by the door who had been so rude was now dozing against the wall. She stepped out cautiously. The other guards were gathered at a wide spot down the hallway, playing cards. She whisked past them without their notice, back to the top of the small stairs.

Another hallway, one she had not entered before, led away from the inner courtyard. She followed it past many doors and up another flight of stairs. Just at the top of these steps she came upon a pair of women in white caps, whispering.

"Grievous sick, for sure," said one. "None has gone into that moat since young Richard, and he was a fool to start with."

"And none has come out of it hale and healthy," said the other. "I am for hot water and cloths."

"And I for the Queen's physician," said the first. "In simple sooth, Master Edward is not like to do better. A sorry day to swim for the both of them, I say."

They stopped speaking when they saw Erica come up behind them.

"My sister," said Erica earnestly. "How is she?"

"You may see for yourself, young mistress," said one, and pointed to a door beside them.

"And shift a skirt while you be at it," the other added. "Lest you catch a death of cold thyself. What meanest thou by not coming up to thy chamber? The banquet is near to begin. Thy parents seek thee."

Erica did not like to be lectured like this. "It's none of your affair," she said curtly. "Go on thy errands before I report you to my mother as useless gossips."

The two women held up their chins and sniffed in affront. But they went their way. Erica had not exactly meant to be cruel. All the same, she felt a little satisfied at having gotten through to them in their own peculiar way of speaking. She was catching on, even without Pedro to help her.

Pedro. Where could he possibly be?

But this was no time to ponder. Now that she had found her room, one that she seemed to share with her supposed sister, she must go in and change out of her ruined clothes. She wondered if she would know what to wear, and if there would be anyone to help her.

Cautiously she slipped in the door and found herself in a wide room with canopied beds on either end. In one of them, Mary lay under quilts and blankets, shivering. For the moment, no one else was in the chamber.

Erica approached the bed and sat down on the edge of it, right next to the shivering girl.

"Are you cold, Mary?" she quietly asked. "It's me, Meg."

There was no response. She didn't even look at her.

Erica stared out a small paned window beside the bed. A full moon, huge and orange in the gathering dusk, was rising over a line of trees. She swallowed hard. It was almost as if the moon were demanding something. The truth, maybe.

"I'm sorry I pushed you in," she said. "Really, I am."

Mary turned and fixed her with a feverish stare.

"Even though I sort of slipped," Erica said. And she paused. "It's just that, well, I was angry. About forgetting what to say in front of the Queen. I couldn't stand it that you kept rubbing it in. But I was wrong. I shouldn't have."

Mary showed a hint of a smile and roused herself. "What a pretty apology thou makest," she whispered. "I am almost of a mind to accept it."

"Oh do, Mary, please do. Then we can be sisters again. You and me, like old times."

Mary sat up a little bit. "I suppose I was put far from loving-kindness—about our turn as fairies of the day and night. But Meg, what meanest thou by 'rubbing it in'? Since when hast thou spoken so newfangledly? Thou hardly seemest thyself today."

Erica could not help smiling. "Oh, Mary. In some ways I do hardly feel myself. Especially today."

"And what be these good old times thou speakest of?" Mary said, shivering in her squeaky voice. "Thou and I never have been sisterly. And yet I would dearly like to be."

"Me too," Erica said. And she felt that she sincerely meant it.

"Thou wouldst?" said Mary.

"I wouldst," said Erica.

Mary put out her trembling hand, and Erica held it.

"When I saw you sink in the moat today," Erica whispered, "I suddenly couldn't bear the thought of losing you. You became—so very precious all of a sudden. So—so—" She lapsed into silence, and they held hands for a long while, watching the moon rise in the window.

"Meg, are you in love with the serving-boy?" Mary said suddenly. "Is he the one that teacheth thee to speak so strangely?"

Erica thought about it a minute. "I don't think so," she finally said. "I don't think I'm in love with him. Not yet, anyway. Perhaps when I am older."

"Thou canst not be," Mary said firmly. "Nor canst thou ever. He is too low for thy station."

"Can you keep a secret?" Erica asked.

Mary nodded.

"He's in disguise. His name is Pedro. His mother is a great scholar from over the sea. He and she know more about our royal Queen than anyone in Hengrave."

"In sooth?" said Mary.

"In simple sooth," said Erica. "But Mary, I have to give you credit. You were right about that man who stopped to speak to us in the carriage today. His name is Charles. Charles Cavendish. His mother wants him to marry me. She's very rich and very greedy. A countess. Just now I overheard her trying to get the Queen's permission. That way Hengrave will eventually belong to her family. She says it would be much better than putting our father in prison."

"As Master Rokewood was put in prison?"

"As Master Rokewood."

"A very wrongful thing," said Mary. "That is what Mother and Father are so afeard of, and why we sought to please the Queen."

"It seems silly to me," said Erica. "This idea of locking up a person in jail and taking his house, just because he wants to go to a different church than you do."

"'Tis no silliness about it," said Mary. "There be only one true church. And our own priests, the holy fathers, do burn at the stake and are hanged and drawn and quartered at the Queen's command. This you well know."

"But what if the Queen believed as we do? Would she burn the Protestants at the stake?"

"Most assuredly, just as the good Queen Mary did when she was alive upon the throne. They be heretics, after all. I wonder you should ask it, Meg."

Erica could see that she was getting nowhere. Mary was looking at her strangely.

"But Meg," she said, in a tone that promised to change the subject.

"Yes?"

"What says the Queen to this proposal?"

"What proposal?"

"The proposal made on behalf of Master Cavendish by his mother the Countess."

"The Queen says nothing, yet."

"But surely, Meg, you will agree to it."

"Mary, oh Mary, please don't!" Erica wailed. "Don't even suggest it. I'm much too young, whatever you say."

"But Meg, thou canst not refuse. 'Twill be the end of Father, and Hengrave, and us all. Dost thou like the man? Dost thou think him well-favored?"

Erica got up off the bed and paced back and forth in silence. Then she stopped.

"Well," she said. "He seems nice enough, I suppose. Though I can't say that I really know him. But he's so old—well into his twenties, I should think—and I'm just thirteen. I'm not even close to ready. It's—Mary, it's ridiculous!"

"Belike you shall be betrothed for a year or twain, not married outright," said Mary quietly.

"Be what?" said Erica.

"Be promised to each other till you come of some older years. Do not play the simpleton, Meg. 'Tis done all the while, as thou well knowest."

Erica thought about this. Perhaps that would be all right. Though she would like to be given more of a choice herself. But what was she thinking? *Herself*? It was Meg that mattered. She wished she could go down to the chapel and tell her the news, give her a chance to make up her own mind. Maybe there would be opportunity.

"Meg?" said Mary softly.

"I'm thinking!" snapped Erica.

"Meg, I was wondering, are you going to play the virginals all by yourself this night? I cannot, and neither can Master Edward, from what I have heard. Dost thou think thou canst?" Mary's voice was getting dreamy.

"I know I canst," Erica said. She sat down on the bed again and squeezed her hand. "Don't worry. Find some sleep. And get well, my dear little sister."

She kissed her on the forehead, and Mary sank back into her bed. Erica tucked a satin quilt under her chin. She looked so peaceful, lying there under the full moon in the window and looking up at her mildly. She didn't seem to be shivering now. Erica bent over her and sang a little snatch of the madrigal, very softly, all in a garden green, and then hummed it, until Mary closed her eyes.

CHAPTER 15

The Banquet

SOON AFTER MARY FELL ASLEEP THE two women servants returned, one with a doctor, another with an armload of hot wet cloths. The Queen's physician had not consented to wait upon them, so they had gone to find "a leech" in the village next door to the manor. When he saw that Mary was resting well, the doctor left to attend on Master Edward, and once again the servants berated Erica for not having dressed. "Just look at you!" This time she let them scold without reply.

She half-expected a warm bath. But after helping her out of her soiled and tattered dress, the servants merely covered her with oils and powders and perfumes, their scent so thick that Erica could scarcely breathe. Then came layer after layer of shifts and kirtles and petticoats, and finally a long-sleeved outer gown that was even more splendid than the one she had gotten from Meg that morning. It was spring green, and they said it perfectly matched her eyes. To Erica's relief it was loose, without any hoops in it. Finally her hair was done up into a coil on top of her head, the way she had seen older girls wear it for a prom or formal. And all was done so swiftly that she hardly believed the transformation.

There was nothing then but to wait for her supposed parents, who were expected any minute to escort her down to the banquet hall. The tall thin serving-boy knocked at the door to announce their imminent arrival. Erica recognized his voice and stepped out cautiously. The women, having finished with her, were now applying hot towels to Mary's forehead. For the moment, they paid no attention to Erica.

"Boy," she said, stepping out into the hallway. "I thank thee for saving my sister's life with the handle of the shovel. I saw thee."

"And I saw thee," he said sullenly.

Erica felt a jolt of shame. "What meanest thou?"

"I saw thee," he merely repeated.

"Wouldst thou do me a favor?" said Erica, a little shaken but nevertheless proud of the way she could speak.

He looked at her without much interest.

"I have gold for thee if thou wilt do what I shall tell thee." Erica didn't know if she had any gold or not, but her promise seemed to have an effect. The boy was suddenly all ears.

"Dost thou recall the musician's servant thou mettest with me in his chamber?"

The boy nodded, and made a grimace. "That scum-face?"

Erica ignored the insult. "He goes by the name of Pedro. Hast thou seen him about of late?"

"I have seen him," said the boy cautiously. "Even now he stayeth by the moat in the outer yard."

Erica smiled at the news. At least he was not wandering about in the woods and fields.

"What I would have thee do is this. Dost thou have a suit of clothes other than the ones thou wearest?"

"But one," said the boy.

"And are they clean?"

"As clean goeth," said the boy.

"It is well," said Erica. "If thou wouldst have gold from me, take that suit and bestow it upon the musician's servant outside the hall. He and thou are of one stature. Wilt thou do this?"

"Aye," said the boy. "For gold I will do it."

"Thou wilt have gold. And when he has put on these clothes, do thou lead him into the hall where he can see the entertainments after the banquet. Place him where he can be seen from the virginals. Wilt thou do this?"

"Aye," said the boy. "For gold I will do it."

"Thou shalt have gold," said Erica.

The serving-boy went off at a run, and Erica smiled. Whatever happened, she wanted Pedro close to her. With him nearby, she knew that she could play her best. And when the time came to find Meg again in her hiding place, she wanted Pedro to go with her.

The serving-boy had no sooner scooted down the stairs than Master Kytson and his wife swept upon her from the upper end of the hallway. They were followed by a host of attendants.

"My dear daughter," said Master Kytson, and kissed her hand.

His wife moved past him and thrust her head into the chamber—as if Erica were not there. She exchanged a few sharp words with the servants attending Mary, then turned back on her husband. "Sick abed, just as I told thee," she hissed. "And Master Edward ill beside. A little water indeed! They might as well have been dipped in poison."

"Most regrettable, dear wife," said Master Kytson. "Extremely regrettable. I own you were right in the matter." He knotted his brow and crossed his arms as if he were protecting himself.

"But Meg," he said, brightening a little. "Thou wilt play for us, wilt thou not? Thou wilt play for us, my girl?"

"With all my heart," said Erica, and gave him a little curtsy in her spring green gown.

"Thou might as well be off to prison now," snapped Mistress Kytson to her husband—"for all this harebrained wench of thine will help thee to a knighthood." She sounded even more sharp than usual. Erica felt a flush of resentment rise in her cheeks.

"Well, well, we shall see," said Master Kytson, doing his best to smooth things over. "Truth is the daughter of time. And more to the purpose, *bon temps viendra*: good times will come. That is the motto of the house. But come, Meg, the feast awaits us."

She followed close behind them, down the steps, down the hallway, and all the way around the inner courtyard to the great stairs, where they ranged themselves on either side to await the Queen's descent from her chamber to the banquet hall. Night had fallen outside the tall windows on the landing, and it seemed the whole manor was ablaze with candles great and small. The Queen's own courtiers waited at the top of the stairs, all newly dressed in brilliant hose and opalescent trousers and jackets that shone in the candlelight. The French ambassadors had dyed their pointed beards and mustaches an exotic array of blues and greens and sulfurous yellows.

All were ready, all were expectant, and just when Erica was beginning to wonder if the Queen would ever come out of her chamber, she appeared among her courtiers at the top of the stairs, followed by her noblewomen and ladies-in-waiting. The Countess of Shrewsbury was closest behind her, dressed in orange taffeta, a grotesque smile on her face. But the Queen's gown outshone them all. It was a deep red velvet, lined with silk, all covered with sewn pearls. Her throat and hair were adorned with jewels of all kinds—rubies and diamonds, sapphires and emeralds—and she held her head as if everyone should know her to be Queen of England whether she wore jewels or not.

As the Queen passed down the stairs, everyone waiting there bowed or curtsied or even kneeled. Then the Kytsons and chief members of their household followed her and her court into the great hall to the roll and flourish of drums and trumpets sounding from the minstrels gallery. Everyone seemed to know his or her place, and there seemed a place for everyone. The Queen sat at a table with her most eminent lords on a raised dais, underneath a great shield carved with the royal coat of arms. The others sat on tables set perpendicularly below. All the tables were spread with rich vermillion cloth, except for the Queen's, which seemed to be a cloth of gold. All of the plate was of richest silver, and overhead a huge branch of copper hung from the high ceiling, holding dozens of thick candles that lit the room as sunrise. The huge hearth was heaped with wood, ready to be lit against the night chill.

Erica took in all of this as she found her seat next to the elder Kytsons. But what she noticed most of all was the double virginal, brought from Master Edward's chamber and placed in the corner next to the dais, just where the grand piano had been—or would be. She wondered when her time would come and felt her fingers trembling; they were more than ready.

And the food. It was a shame she could hardly eat a bite of it. After the Queen's chaplain offered a formal blessing read from a book, the servants brought in heaping platters of meat and fish and pitchers dripping with savory sauces, sometimes accompanied by musical sallies of fifes and hoboys. Aside from a giant pig's head, stuffed with an apple, Erica would not have known what any of it was, really, except that people sitting nearby kept complimenting Meg's father and mother on the beef and mutton and veal and lamb, on the goose and capon and rabbit and turkey, on the mallard and swan and crane and pigeon, on the plover and pheasant and partridge and quail—and on more birds she had never heard of. And she also heard compliments on the sturgeon and crayfish and oysters and anchovies, the pike and carp and perch and herring. There were Holland cheeses and Yorkshire puddings and something sweet called marchpane, there were baskets and baskets of good white bread with creamy butter, and over and over there were loud calls for beer and ale and white wine and malmsey and claret and sack with vinegar. And none of it seemed in short supply. Erica had never seen such an abundance of food and drink in her whole life, and believed she never would again.

And the more the company ate and drank, the merrier they all became, until even the Queen was laughing wholeheartedly at things her courtiers happened to say (things that everyone else in the hall pretended to hear so that they could laugh along with the Queen). All the while the musicians played sweetly in the gallery on the viols and the violins, even though they could hardly be noted over the noise of talk and shouting.

As the evening drew on and on, Erica began to wonder how much longer the feast could last. For a good while she had been looking about for Pedro, dressed in the serving-boy's spare clothes. She hoped she would see him bringing in a pitcher of wine, or standing in a door or a corner. But look as she would, she could not find him. It was getting late—she was starting to feel so tired and nervous all at once. If only he would make an appearance.

At last all of the food and dishes and silverware were cleared from the tables, the fire was lit, and everyone sat back on their benches with goblets of drink still in their hands. There was a general consensus of quiet. A musician dressed in black came down from the gallery and played a lute song next to the hearth. It was something soft and beautiful. He sang all about how he would play his lute no longer because his lady loved him no more:

The Banquet

My lute, awake! Perform the last
Labor that thou and I shall waste,
And end that I have now begun;
For when this song is sung and past,
My lute, be still, for I have done.

Erica still kept looking about the room for Pedro. No Pedro. All she saw this time was Charles Cavendish, smiling at her from where he stood near a door at the far side of the hall. He was wearing yellow cross-gartered stockings that made him stand out in the crowd. She wondered that she had not seen him before this. His blonde curls looked strikingly handsome and pleasant in the candlelight, but Erica was not sure she wanted to see him just now. He made her nervous, and what she needed now more than anything was to be calm.

When the lute song was over the Queen smiled and clapped her hands politely, and everyone else did likewise. Then suddenly Master Kytson arose and nodded in turn to everyone present, as if it were he that had played the lute and were now receiving their general congratulations.

"Your grace," he said, bowing to the Queen. "Your noble lordships. Knights and ladies all. You do me honor to sup with me in my small house. Be assured, all Hengrave thanks you. If my father yet were here, who built this hall and served the good King Henry the Eighth as well as I seek to serve the royal Queen his daughter, his gratitude and pleasure would be no less full than mine at present. The hour grows late for your grace and your lordships. But before you betake yourselves to rest, indulge us a last slight entertainment. A young daughter of mine doth wish to play a measure or two on the Queen's chosen instrument. Whether she hath been well taught I leave to your better judgments, and most of all, to your gracious majesty's."

Meg's father bowed to the Queen. Then he knotted his brow and looked at Erica and nodded. As he sat down, he wrapped both hands around his goblet as if in prayer.

Chapter 16

Four Hands, Two Voices

ERICA WALKED TO THE VIRGINAL IN the midst of a precarious silence. She was conscious of the eyes upon her, especially those of Charles Cavendish. As she approached the dais she could clearly see that Queen Elizabeth wore a smile perhaps more playful than proud. The Queen seemed to nod her head. Erica felt suddenly heartened, and dropped a curtsy before the dais as elaborately as she knew how.

At the double virginal she took her seat on the empty bench and found her music propped before her. Strange—she had not even thought to worry about having or missing the musical score. Perhaps she even had it by heart. But no, she had the music and she would use it. She straightened the bench, straightened the score, and put her hands to the keys—or *jacks*. Pedro had told her they were jacks. But why was she thinking of keys and jacks? She was supposed to be playing now. Would she sing too? She hadn't thought about this, either. Perhaps she would. But what was a madrigal with only one voice? She would only sing if the playing went very well, perhaps the second or third time through.

Here—she had considered enough. It was time to begin.

Her fingers pressed down on the jacks. For the first few notes they felt numb and thick and terribly wrong. But then the very tips of her fingers suddenly remembered themselves. The strings sounded, humming and plucking in quick succession, the playful formality that was the essence of madrigal, the then that was now. She felt the hall fill with the sureness and lightness of the music, the quick-and-gone delight of it, and as she went on, she approached each passage more daringly, more trippingly, until she did not think of the possibility of hitting a single note in error. She felt a smile grow on her face, knew for certain that what she enjoyed, others were enjoying. She felt regret when she realized she was almost halfway through the score. She was flying, she was soaring, she was playing dancing maidens and golden apples and blonde-haired gods and gardens of goodness and—

"Stop!" cried the Queen.

Erica could not believe her ears, but her fingers fell from the virginal and landed trembling in her lap. What oh what oh what had she done?

"Is that not a double pair of virginals thou playest?" asked the Queen, looking directly at Erica.

"Yes, your majesty," Erica whispered.

"And is that not a score for two pair of hands that thou playest?"

"Yes, your majesty," Erica tried to say again, but her throat was dry, and all she could really do was nod.

"Hast thou no one to play it with thee?" the Queen asked.

"Yes—I mean no, your grace," said Erica, finding her voice. "I was supposed to play with my sister, but she fell in the moat, and now she is very ill. Which is my fault, really, because I sort of pushed her, because she made so much fun of me after I forgot what to say to your majesty when we were fairies, if your majesty remembers."

A light ripple of laughter had begun to cross the hall as she spoke. Some people, when they are nervous, say too little, and others, sometimes, say too much. Erica suddenly realized what she was doing and blushed with shame. But the Queen held up her hand, and the laughter stopped.

"Thou hast no one else with whom to play?"

"Well," said Erica, unable to help herself, "Master Edward, of course, my teacher, but he jumped in the moat to save my sister this afternoon and almost drowned, so now he is sick too—because of what's in the moat, I guess—and I'm trying to do the best I can all by myself because, well, you are the Queen, you know, and you don't come to Hengrave every day and we want to make a good impression."

She stopped when she heard the tittering begin again. She looked out and saw Meg's father bending down with his face in his hands.

"Thou dost excellently alone," the Queen pronounced, and everyone was silent again. "But thou wouldst do even more excellently with a partner in practice. I think I recognize the piece. It is 'All in a Garden Green,' is it not?"

Erica nodded.

"Very well," said the Queen. "We our royal self shall join you."

We? thought Erica. Who is *we?* But then she saw the Queen herself, and no one else, arise from the dais and step down to the virginal. Everyone in the hall stood up, and Erica did too, to be safe. No one sat down again until the Queen took her seat on the bench next to Erica.

"Be seated, child. Be not afraid." The way she said it, and even something about the way the Queen looked, reminded Erica instantly of Sister Julian, and filled her with a sudden courage.

She sat elbow to elbow with the Queen, her spring green gown against the royal red velvet and white satin sewn with dozens and dozens of pearls, and thought to herself, she's just a woman. She's just a woman about to play the virginal, as I am. Erica took the sheaf of music and propped it directly in front of the Queen. "I don't need it," she whispered. "I pretty much know it by heart."

The Queen studied the music attentively, and Erica studied the Queen. Close up, her eyes looked even more quick and intelligent than from a distance. She watched them scan the notes in a knowing way, learning them in quick glances. Her red hair looked thin and brittle, her forehead frail. And yet, and yet, this was the Queen.

Erica closed her eyes and then opened them and looked about her to clear her mind, to be ready to play the music again. Not far from her, standing near the fire, was a young man, a boy, with a lute. She blinked and stared. The boy was Pedro, dressed in a coarse blue livery that actually fit. He smiled at her.

The Queen nodded at Erica. "One matter more," she said in a low voice. "Can you sing? If so, we need one person more to bear the burden, for I cannot. A madrigal is best with voices."

"I can sing," Erica quavered uncertainly.

"As can I, your majesty," Pedro said, strolling over to their side and laying down his lute on the floor. He bowed to the Queen expertly.

Erica could hardly keep her jaw from dropping. She had never heard him sing before. What in the world did he think he was doing? All the same, it was a comfort to feel him approach. This time, no one cuffed him away, though several lords rose from the dais and glared at him for his boldness.

"He is more than he seems, your majesty," Erica whispered. "The son of a great scholar from Spain and a worthy apprentice to our Musician-in-Chief."

The Queen appraised him coolly. "Very well," she finally said. She nodded at her lords to be seated and turned again to the virginal. Pedro stepped behind them to where he could see the music, hands clasped behind his back.

"Then let us begin," said the Queen. She gave Erica a little nod and both of them breathed in at once.

Erica's fingers touched the jacks just a little ahead of the Queen's, but then she slowed and waited for her, realizing that in her excitement she might play at a faster pace than the Queen was capable of. For all she knew, the Queen was sight-reading the piece for the first time. But to her surprise, her partner soon caught up to her and even began to overtake her. She was a better player than Erica could have imagined. And the message from the Queen was clear: she was a woman who liked to be first. Erica took pains to let her dominate the melody.

But after a while it didn't matter. One became used to the other, and Erica felt the Queen allowing their hands to merge in synchrony. The sound was good and rich and full, just as it had been with Master Edward in his chamber and, in a way, as it had been with Pedro on the grand piano in this same room at some point in the recent past or distant future. As one run replaced another in counterpoint upon counterpoint, she felt the Queen occasionally look over at her with a wry smile, as if she were enjoying herself. In fact, there was no *as if* about it. Together they were making music.

They finished the madrigal one time through, and then the Queen whispered to them, "Now add thy voices. Hold nothing back."

Erica began her part, quavery and weak at first but finding her range, finding the fullness of her throat. And then suddenly Pedro was there, singing behind them as Master Edward had sung before. *All in a garden green, two lovers sat at ease. . . .* He could sing, he could sing! How he could sing! . . . *as they could scarce be seen among, among the leafy trees.* She had not known he had it in him. The Queen looked up and whispered to her, "Thou art the veriest pair of nightingales I ever did hear."

And so her hands raced with the Queen's, and her voice ran sweet and wild in tangles, in and out of Pedro's

singing. There were many verses to the song about the
good and faithful lovers, and the three of them went on
and on, repeating and repeating the stanzas till Erica was
hardly conscious of any plan or felt design in what they
did. They were just singing. They were just playing. And
they were inside a living moment of palpable beauty
where popes and priests and Protestants and princes and
prisons didn't matter. They didn't matter the least little bit
in the realm of music the three were creating. And neither
did the future or past, or the fact that one of them played
the role of a queen and one of an heiress and one of a
lowly serving-boy. Or that one was English and two were
now American. Or that one was old and two were young.
Or that one was dead and two alive, or one alive and two
unborn. Because they were all molded together in an on-
going musical pattern, melded in a continuous maze.

All the while that Erica was singing and playing she
did not exactly think these things but felt them deeply, felt
them in ear and flesh and bone. Afterward she believed
that it was this more than anything that she had been sent
to know and learn. Although, if you asked her what "this"
was, she would simply drop her hands to her sides and
say, "You know, *the music*. With Pedro. And the Queen."

At long last, after they had repeated the madrigal
more times than they could tell, the Queen nodded to
both of them and let her hands jump from the jacks on a
final chord, and Erica with her. She expected to hear some
kind of applause. But there was none. Instead there was a
profound silence. There are silences of embarrassment or
uncertainty, when no one applauds because he or she is

afraid of being the only one. But this was not that kind of silence. It was, rather, the deep quiet of appreciation, the silence in which no one applauds because any applause is unnecessary, because everyone is so moved by what he or she has heard that to clap hands is to break a spell, to ruin a charm, to put out the light before its time.

It soon became clear that if anyone was to break the silence, it would have to be the Queen. And finally she did.

"Thomas Kytson," she called out in her high, firm, piping voice. "Approach our presence and kneel before us."

Meg's father stood up, evidently in a daze, and everyone else stood up too, for so had the Queen. He shuffled to the virginal where the Queen waited with Pedro and Erica by her side. Meanwhile, at a nod from the Queen, one of her courtiers handed her a long ceremonial sword with silver blade and golden hilt. Meg's father sank on one knee before her, head raised.

"Thomas Kytson," said the Queen in a loud voice, "for thy many loyal services offered unto this our crown, and for thy faithfully rendered obedience to our royal person, we make thee knight of the realm."

Then she held the hilt of the sword with both hands and lightly touched him with the blade on one shoulder and then the other.

Well, thought Erica, better than cutting off someone's head.

"Sir Thomas Kytson, rise," she commanded.

And he did. The second he was on his feet, the hall burst into ear-deafening applause. He smiled shyly, apparently muttered his thanks to her majesty, though Erica could not hear them, and shambled back to his bench at his table, more dazed than when he had left it. The applause went on and on and on. Good enough for something like this, Erica thought. Not for the music, but for this sort of worldly honor, just right.

As the clapping and shouting died down, Erica started to follow Sir Kytson back to their table. Pedro, she noticed, had already picked up his lute and vanished back into a throng of servants beside the hearth. But as Erica stepped from the virginal the Queen held out her hand to stop her.

"Nay, Margaret Kytson. Stay. For you as well, we have something to give thee," the Queen said aloud. "An honorable household such as that of Sir Thomas here should live in perpetuity. It wants heirs. Not every woman can live and prosper in solitary singleness. And as for Hengrave, it must be peopled!"

A few of the men dared to laugh, and some of the ladies-in-waiting tittered. But Erica was most uneasy.

"Therefore it is our royal pleasure," said the Queen, "to this very night approve your betrothal, with the kind permission and ready assent of thy loyal parents, to the youngest son of our dear Countess of Shrewsbury."

A murmur ran through the assembly.

"Charles Cavendish, be pleased to approach our presence."

Erica stood and gaped miserably at the blonde young man who walked—no, floated—toward her. When he came before the Queen, he kneeled—yellow cross-gartered stockings and all—and kissed her hand. Then she took Erica's hand with her own right hand and Charles' in her own left hand and held them inches apart, as if ready to join them together.

"Charles Cavendish," said the Queen, "dost thou, before these present, promise to betroth thyself to Margaret Kytson, and to marry her when time, her sovereign, and her parents do allow?"

"I do so promise," he said, smiling. He was smiling right at Erica.

You're making a big mistake, she wanted to tell him.

But now the Queen was speaking again. "Margaret Kytson, dost thou before these witnesses covenant to betroth thyself to Charles Cavendish, and to marry him when time, his sovereign, and his mother do allow?"

There was silence again in the room. This time it was a silence of expectancy, a waiting and hoping for something to happen. So recently, Erica had experienced the most wonderful silence of her life. And now, just minutes later, she was living through the most miserable one. Everyone in the room, she felt sure—everyone except Pedro, that is—wanted her to say yes to the Queen, to agree to a promise of betrothal. And she couldn't very well say no. Not for Meg. Not for herself. They were both trapped, neither of them given a choice.

So she would have to give in. Or she would have to explain. One or the other. She couldn't just say no.

"Young Margaret, dost thou so promise and covenant?" the Queen asked again, looking at her very directly. "Be not afraid to speak."

This gave her courage. She would say it. She would speak for herself. Erica slowly opened her mouth. She was about to get the word out—which one, she didn't know.

But suddenly, a high clear voice like her own rang out across the hall. "No!" it cried. "For by my life, that be not Margaret Kytson!"

The Queen dropped her hand in surprise. Everyone was looking up at the minstrels gallery, which had long been deserted by the musicians, who had gone downstairs to the kitchen to eat. There in the front row stood a girl with dusty auburn hair who was wrapped in a sheet from the linen closet. Poking out from the top of the sheet were Erica's baby-blue suspenders. Their eyes met. Erica smiled weakly.

It was Margaret, of course. And she was not smiling in return.

Chapter 17

Time to Leave

THE QUEEN LOOKED FROM MARGARET to Erica, and from Erica to Margaret, and back again. So did Charles Cavendish. So did Sir Thomas Kytson and his wife. So did they all. The Queen's lip trembled. Charles quivered. Sir Thomas and his wife crossed themselves. Everyone else began to murmur.

"Peace!" the Queen called at last. Then she pointed to the girl in the gallery. "If thou beest mortal flesh underneath thy winding sheet, speak on. If not, doom and curses now betide thee."

"I am most woefully abused!" shouted Meg. "And can prove every word I say." She drew herself up to a full and shivering height behind the parapet, and the room broke into a murmur again.

The Queen held up her hand for silence. "Say on," she commanded.

"This girl," said Meg, pointing beneath her, "who appeareth like me in every feature, came as I thought in answer to prayer as heaven sent. As I have no skill upon the virginals, and was sore afraid of playing before your majesty, so I wept and prayed in the chapel this morning, and this young woman, who will answer to the name of Erica, appeared to me in the gallery, just as I appear to you in this gallery now. She heard my woes and promised to play for me this night. From whence she came I know not, and she says not, but now in my heart I fear to think. In foolish haste I gladly accepted her offer of help, and we exchanged our garments—mine for her outlandish and immodest dress, as here I do hope to conceal—and I have hid me all the day until she should fulfill her promise. And then, after the night wore on, and no sign of this Erica, who had promised to return to me, I crept out from my place of hiding and found a way to this gallery, now to find her stealing a husband where I thought her merely to be making music in my stead. I do confess what I have done, and my deserving of reprimand and punishment. But as for this dark visitor, I fain would know what she deserveth!"

This speech had a remarkable effect. Some cried out, "Demon! Witchcraft!" and pointed at Erica. Others pointed at Meg in the gallery and shouted the same. After all, she was the one who was wrapped in a sheet. Still others said they had known the music they had heard was neither human nor natural. Only the devil could bring such sounds from a virginal. An angel, rather, others insisted. The Kytsons kept crossing themselves. Charles Cavendish drew away from Erica in bewildered horror, melting back into the crowd. Pedro, meanwhile, edged toward her bit by bit, since no one was watching him. And the Queen, after dropping her hand, kept a firm hold on her shoulder. Angel or demon, she was afraid of neither one.

The hubbub grew until the Queen gathered her wits and called out, "Silence! We shall determine in this case."

In a few moments the room was quiet. She held Erica at arm's length and commanded, "Margaret Kytson—or Erica—what say you to this charge and to this person?"

Everyone waited for her to speak. But instead of addressing the Queen, she turned her face to the girl in the gallery. "Meg, I didn't mean to," she said. "Really, I didn't. No one gave me a choice."

But the last parts of what she said were completely lost in the noise and confusion which erupted when she addressed the girl above her as Meg. For of course that meant that she herself was not Meg, but someone or something else—an imposter.

"Burn her!" cried one.

"Off with her head!

"A succubus!"

"A spirit!"

"The devil!"

Erica felt Pedro's hand clasp her own. The Queen kept her grasp on her shoulder.

"It's all a mistake!" she cried out. "I'm not something evil at all! I'm just a girl!"

But no one heard her—the noise in the hall was too great. Men had climbed up on the tables and handed Meg down into the hall from the gallery. She was weeping in her father's arms. Lady Kytson looked very angry. The Countess of Shrewsbury looked very angry. Even the Queen looked as if she might lose her temper at any minute.

"We've got to get out of here," Pedro whispered. "Where can we run?"

Before Erica could think of an answer a new sound came to her ears. It was the sound of two dogs barking. Not just any dogs, but big dogs, huge dogs, dogs like— well, she couldn't place them, exactly. Suddenly, through the two doors under the gallery—the doors that said *Fear God* and *Honor the King*—a pair of the largest, friendliest, slobberiest St. Bernards came loping in, crashing into the covered tables and knocking them off their trestles onto the gathered guests. The sound of their barking filled the room with animal joy. Erica was quite sure she had seen them before.

Right after the dogs came a strong grizzled man with a rake, a young red-headed boy, and an even younger little girl.

Erica put her hand to her mouth.

"Ho, Meg! Ho, Mary!" called the man, waving his rake in agitation. "What are ye getting yourselves into? As ever I was born—ye know ye are to stay outside. Look now at all these ladies and gentlemen ye be disturbin'."

But the dogs went romping onward, pulling rich red tablecloths behind them in a clatter and crash of pitchers and goblets.

The boy was close on the heels of the man. He seemed to be chasing the dogs as well, but appeared to be much less concerned with the chaos that they were causing. The more of a romp, the better. Behind him trailed the dark-haired little girl, innocently along for the ride.

The dogs flew past the virginal and mounted up along the dais, creating more havoc as they went. The man, the boy, and the girl came running right behind them.

"Edward!" called Erica. "Walter! Katrina! Where are you going?"

Suddenly the three of them stopped. The Queen looked rather interested.

"Hey, Erica!" Walter called. "The dogs got into the kitchen. We're trying to catch them! You need to help us!" He looked around, taking in the scene more carefully. "So . . . this some kind of costume party?"

Katrina put out her hand to hold the Queen's red velvet gown. "Oooh," she said. "Pretty dress!"

Edward looked about nervously and decided to address the Queen. "Begging your pardon, ma'am," he said, setting his rake across his shoulder as if he were holding a rifle at attention, "but do I remember you as being one of the Sisters of the Assumption?"

For a moment it looked as if the Queen were about to become terribly angry. But then she let go Erica's shoulder and sent up peals of laughter that went echoing into the rafters of the great hall. It was more than even she could take.

Erica didn't stay to see what would happen when the Queen stopped laughing. "Let's go, now!" she called out to the others.

The dogs had completed their demolition of the dais and bounded out the entrance of the great hall. Before anyone could stop them, Erica grabbed Walter's hand, Pedro grabbed Katrina's, and all of them followed Edward after the St. Bernards at top speed across the front of the head table. Together they flew out the entrance, past the foot of the great stairs, down the long hallway and smack through the doors of the chapel. Whether the dogs were leading them there—or Edward, or fate—Erica never afterward knew. She heard voices behind her calling, "After them! Seize the witch!"

They tumbled down the aisle to the altar and paused beneath the stained-glass windows, glowing now in the moonlight. Walter grabbed the dogs and said, "Now where do we go? And what's going on, Erica?"

"In here," she said, crossing to the secret panel and pressing along the bottom of it in desperation. "There's no time, Walter! There's no time!"

The panel opened to her touch.

"Cool!" said Walter.

"Get in!" said Erica. "Everyone, get in! Get in!"

Obedient for once, Meg and Mary bounded through the open panel, and Walter eagerly crawled in after.

"Isn't it sort of dark in there?" Katrina asked.

But Erica shoved her inside, and Pedro and Edward came along quickly behind, shutting the panel neatly behind them. They were all crammed in the narrow space. It was utterly dark.

"There are stairs," whispered Erica. "Steep steps in the back. They curve round and round in a spiral. It's the only way."

Groping and bumping and banging their heads against each other, they finally got the dogs headed up the stairs. Erica found her face planted firmly into the furry behind of a St. Bernard. "C'mon, Meg," she said. "Or Mary—or whoever you are." And they pushed and strained and crawled and struggled up the steps in the pitch dark. Finally the dogs would not move any further, and Erica reached up past her dog and felt solid stone over her head.

Great, she thought. But she didn't give up. She worked her hand over the stone and pushed and pried until suddenly she felt it come loose, like a rock rolled away from a tomb. There was a hole overhead, and light. The dog poked its way through and clambered out. Then Erica. She was standing in a small room by a bathtub. Of course! she said to herself. The privy. The privy in the turret of the corner chamber, just as Margaret had said. Strange, though, how familiar this bathtub looked on its four clawed feet. And the washbasin. And the mirror. All glowing silver and white in the moonshine through the small windows.

More light came from the adjacent chamber. The door was ajar. The dog had already bounded through it. There was her father, sitting at the small round table in a large nest of books and papers. So focused. Not looking up. But the dog had seen him. The dog was bounding into his lap with unmeasured joy. And her father was down, the table was down, his papers flying everywhere.

Another St. Bernard came wriggling out of the hole behind her and bolted past. Then Walter, and Pedro, and Katrina, and Edward, still somehow holding onto his rake.

Erica stepped into the chamber. Her poor father was flat on his back, Meg and Mary licking his face and barking with a wild abandon, as if they had finally found their quarry.

"Shoo," she said. "You, get off!"

The dogs ran out the door to the hall, and the others gathered on either side of Erica.

Her father sat up.

"Hi, Dad," she said. And she smiled.

CHAPTER 18

Ever After

I T WAS NOT A LONG AUTUMN AFTER ALL. Though Erica could not exactly say she loved to be in England, she found she did not hate it either. Sometimes they all went to museums in London, or on hikes in the Lake District, or to plays in Stratford-upon-Avon. But most of the time they remained at Hengrave Hall. The four of them would have school with Mrs. Pickins in the corner library every morning. Then, after a late lunch, if the weather were nice, Katrina and Walter would go outside to romp with the dogs, and Erica, whatever the weather, would practice on the piano in the great hall. Pedro always came to listen, and often lay on his back on the floor, hidden beneath the sounding wires. Sometimes, if a voice were called for, he would stand behind her and sing.

Erica often told him how surprised she had been that first time he had sung with her on the night of the feast. Pedro said it surprised him too—but he had volunteered because just that spring, when he had joined the school choir on a dare, the director had said he had a nice voice, a good tenor voice, and some of the girls had agreed. So maybe he could sing after all. Also, he felt sorry for the Queen, who said she couldn't. As for his lute, he had found it leaning against a wall outside the kitchen, and thought it would make a good disguise. Most of the extra musicians were hired strangers anyway. The rest, he said, was history.

Walter and Katrina never seemed quite aware of their brief visit to the past. Katrina kept telling her mother about the woman in the pretty dress. Dr. Lopez, however, was much too busy with her studies in Elizabethan clothing as a sign system to take notice. Walter spent an extraordinary amount of time in their corner bathroom, trying to find the stone in the floor that lifted out, but he never did. He only succeeded in making his mother worry about his English diet and in making his father late for class.

Edward would say nothing at all about what happened except for the strange things a full moon could do to a person. For a full moon it had been—a blue moon in fact, the second full moon of the month—and Walter and Katrina had been given permission to run about with the dogs on the lawn late at night. This was only because Sister Julian claimed she had taken Pedro and Erica to visit a family in distress—and that they had stayed for a late supper. Erica's mother, who believed in absolutely everything that Sister Julian said or did, was satisfied with this explanation and had convinced Pedro's mother to be satisfied as well. The upshot was that Walter and Katrina had begged to stay up also, and had thus been allowed to join Edward and the St. Bernards outside the manor. On their way back in through the kitchen door, the dogs had somehow gotten in too, and then the chase.

It was strange what a full moon—a blue moon, even—could do to one's sense of time and place.

And on that night, Erica's father did not take particular notice of Erica's gown or Pedro's worsted livery—perhaps he thought that they had been playing dress-up again with the costumes from the minstrels gallery. Mr. Pickins did not even take much notice of the fact that two dogs and five people had suddenly emerged from the bathroom. He had been so immersed in his grading and lecture preparation that for all he knew they had come in through the main door of the chamber. He did not know from which direction the dogs had come that knocked him over—and once knocked over, he did not know where Erica and the others had arrived from either. Her mother was the kind of person who would have noticed, but she had been downstairs in the tearoom with Dr. Lopez, keeping an eye on the children, who were just outside the window on the back lawn with Edward and the St. Bernards in the moonlight. So there had been very little after all for Erica to explain. Her mother did remark, a few days later, that her baby-blue denims were missing, and all Erica could do was agree that she wished she knew where they were. "They can't have gone far," her mother always said.

Of course, Pedro and Erica often talked about their adventures, though they had no wish to repeat them. For the rest of the autumn Erica refused to venture into the chapel, no matter how beautiful the singing there. And neither of them felt like watching the television in the Wilbye Chamber. But they did wonder how things had gone on in Hengrave after the visit of the Queen. Erica thought of the tall thin serving-boy who never got his promised gold and lost a suit of clothes in the bargain. Most of all, she wondered whether Meg and Mary ever did become friends, and whether Meg did indeed marry Charles Cavendish.

Sometimes she would ask Sister Julian about these things—cautiously, as if she were merely interested in the history of Hengrave. But the nun would answer, "Peace, Erica—you did what you were called to do. We are seldom given to know the consequences of our efforts. It is enough to have been and done; we leave the rest to Providence."

But Erica would not leave off asking, and so one rainy afternoon, Sister Julian led her out the side of the hall and across a wet and leaf-strewn lawn.

"Where are we going?" Erica asked.

Sister Julian said nothing, but guided her through the wind and showers to the door of the church with the small round tower.

"Why are we coming here?" said Erica. She had not gone into the church before. Somehow it had felt off-limits.

Sister Julian straightened her wimple and lifted the latch. A gust of wind nudged them inside the door, and it slammed shut behind them. Erica stood very still. The church was not at all large, but it held a quiet that was huge. The rain echoed off the roof and created a soft musical hush. In the dim light, she saw the place was full of tombs and monuments. Carven figures lay atop the tombs on their backs, hands pressed together in prayer. To all appearances, this was a church for the dead.

Sister Julian led her to a corner and stopped. They were standing in front of a pillared canopy shaped from stone. Underneath lay three prone figures side by side. The one in the middle was a man dressed in a suit of armor; the two on either side were women in large ruffs and cockleshell hats. At their feet kneeled a stag and a unicorn, and below their heads were the carved stone figures of two young women, kneeling as well.

There was lettering on the side of the tomb, but Erica found it hard to read. "Who are these people?" she whispered.

"The one in armor represents Sir Thomas Kytson the Younger," answered Sister Julian. "On either side are his two wives."

"His *two* wives?" Erica asked.

"Yes, the first one died almost the day she was married. The second one, Elizabeth, was mother to the two daughters shown on the side of the tomb.

Erica looked harder at the faces in effigy ranged before her—so somber, so very composed, and not at all as Erica remembered them.

"Elizabeth is the one the Queen put into prison," Sister Julian said softly. "Not Sir Thomas after all. It happened ten years after the Queen's visit. She wouldn't give up on the old faith."

Erica nodded. She could believe it. Those two Elizabeths were bound to collide someday.

"What about the two daughters?" Erica asked. She tried to sound casual about it.

"Neither one is buried here," the nun said, "but both are mentioned in the inscription." She stooped in the dim light, marking the words with her finger so that Erica could follow along as she read aloud:

> *Here lyeth the body of Sir Thomas Kytson,*
> *Knight, first married to Jane, one of the*
> *daughters of the Lord Pagett, who dying without*
> *issue, he next married Elizabeth,*
> *the eldest daughter of Sir Thomas Cornewalleis,*
> *Knight, by whom he had one sonne,*
> *that died in his infancie,*
> *and two daughters, Margaret and Mary; the*
> *first married to Sir Charles Cavendish, Knight—*

Erica reached out and caught the nun's finger, interrupting its slow progress. "So she did marry him," she whispered.

"Yes," said Sister Julian. "Margaret Kytson became Lady Cavendish four years after the Queen's progress."

"She was only seventeen," said Erica as if to herself. "Seventeen when she got married."

"Perhaps," said Sister Julian, "though we can't be sure. There exists no exact record of her birth."

Erica smiled, pleased to know an intimate secret from the past. But Sister Julian looked at her sadly. Erica suddenly felt uncertain.

"And then?" she asked.

"And then," Sister Julian said, "she died only a year later, giving birth to her first child, who perished with her. It was terribly common in those days—both to marry young and to die young."

Erica stared fixedly at the kneeling figures on the tomb. A life cut short, she thought, fallen into the waiting moat. A precious life much like her own. She felt her eyes begin to burn.

"And Mary?" she asked, hurrying to change the subject.

"Married to a powerful earl," Sister Julian told her. "And then very cruelly divorced. A bitter woman in the end. Of her marriage she always said afterward, 'If not, I care not.'"

To Erica, the words sounded oddly familiar.

Then a dark feeling rose inside her, as if notes and voices were being erased. "It's not fair!" she wailed. Erica began to weep. The rain kept falling on the roof as if it were trying to quiet her.

"Oh no," said Sister Julian after a space. "It's never fair. No one ever said it would be. Even the Queen died very unhappy—she never got to marry at all."

"Neither have you," said Erica impulsively. She suddenly felt as if she were in an argument.

"But that's by choice, dear. I happen to believe in—well—music, you could call it. Yes, music."

She took Erica's hand in her own and led her back to the door of the church. They paused there and turned again to regard the tomb in its dim corner. Erica was still sniffling.

"We are Kytsons all," the old nun said quietly. "*Bon temps viendra*, Erica. Good times will come."

Sister Julian opened the door, and for the moment the rain had stopped. Leaves were flying in the wind, and the walls of Hengrave rose before them, glistening. From the other side of the manor came a deep and welcome set of echoes. Erica lifted an ear. It was the sound of two dogs barking, as if in time.

CHAPTER 19

And After That

ERICA FOUND HER WAY BACK INTO THE great hall, back to the ebony grand piano, and sat on the bench quietly for a long time, listening to a resurgence of the rain and the wind. She put her fingers to the keys, but they rested there without moving.

Pedro, she thought. She needed Pedro.

As if summoned by wish, Pedro sashayed through the door with an old ledger in his hands. He pointed up to the tall bay window and said, "You won't believe this, Erica, but I just read in the household expense book—a very old book that Sister Julian loaned to me—that this entire window had to be replaced, at an expense of ten shillings, after it was—here, let me read it—after it was 'shaken down by the discharging of a gun or two in the time of Christmas, 1572.' Imagine that. Wild times, eh? And ten shillings. That was a lot in those days."

This was not the Pedro she needed, and the look on her face must have told him so.

"What's the matter, Erica?" Pedro said.

She made no reply.

"Play a little something, would you?" He sat down on the bench beside her, uninvited.

She took her hands off the keys and folded them in her lap.

"Pedro," she said quietly, "what is it with your needing to know all these things?"

"What do you mean?" Pedro said. His own hands took a grip on his knees.

"I mean, why is it you have this need to master all this obscure information? Who is it you are trying to impress?"

"Impress?" he said.

"Yes, because it's not me," Erica said.

"You?" said Pedro.

"Stop being such a parrot," she said.

"Parrot?"

"Stop it!"

Pedro stared into the distance.

"It's your father, isn't it?"

"What do you mean?" Pedro said again. But now his hands were trembling.

"Your dad, he's a professor like your mom, right?"

"Right," said Pedro. "A distinguished chair of medieval studies at the University of—"

Erica cut him off. "And really smart like your mom, right?"

"Yes," he said, "really smart."

"But he's gone, right? He doesn't live with you guys anymore."

"He visits!" said Pedro. "But he and mom couldn't get a job at the same—"

"Still," said Erica. "He's not here, is he? Haven't seen him, anyway."

Oh, that was cruel, she thought. But somehow she didn't care.

Pedro shook his head. Then he looked slowly away, out the window, and swiped a hand under one eye.

"You know what I think?" said Erica. "I think you think that if you are just smart enough, and memorize enough odd things, your father will come around more often. I think you are trying to earn his respect. His love, even. And I think you need to stop it, Pedro. You really do. You really need to just be you."

Pedro shifted his gaze from the window to the paneled wall.

Then, in a whisper, she added, "I would like you a lot better."

Did I just say that? she thought.

"And so would your father," she went on. "Not that he doesn't already like you. Of course he does. And so do I. He didn't leave because you were dumb. And he won't come back because you're smart. And if you stop acting so smart, I won't feel so dumb."

Erica felt her throat catch, her eyes moisten. The rain and the wind beat upon the tall bay window like a piece of music sprung loose from time.

Pedro turned back to her. There were real tears on his face. "Okay," he said. "Okay. Okay. You might be right, Erica. You really, really might be right."

"Pedro, I'm sorry. I shouldn't have—"

"No, you should. I'm glad you did. My mom is great, but I really do miss my dad. And I—"

"I like you just the way you are, Pedro," Erica said. "Really, I do."

And did I just say that, too? she thought.

"But I think you're on to something, Erica. Something true. Some part of me thinks that if I am the perfect little scholar then my father will come back home again. And I'm a little bit tired of it. A lot, actually."

Erica gave him a little smile.

"But," said Pedro, taking one hand from his knee and placing it lightly atop her own, "as long as we're talking about these things, I have a question for you."

"A question?" sniffled Erica.

"Stop being a parrot," he said.

"Parrot?" she said. Truth be told, she liked the soft feeling of his hand on her knee. Better than those cold stone monuments in the church with Sister Julian.

"My question is, who are you playing your music for, Erica?"

"*Hmm,*" she said. "Maybe the Queen?"

"Not anymore," said Pedro. "That's over, I think."

"Over?" she said. "It won't ever be over, Pedro. Even if we never go back."

"Which I don't think we will," he said.

"Maybe," she said. "Hard to tell." But she knew he was probably right.

"So right here, right now, who do you play for, Erica?"

It's now or never, Erica thought. And she carefully covered the hand that was on her knee with her own.

"For you, Pedro," Erica said, in what she hoped was her softest voice. But she sounded as squeaky as Mary Kytson, talking to her ducks in the moat.

"Flattered, I'm sure," Pedro said. "But who else?"

Erica drew her hand away. She had made her offer— a good one, she thought—and been refused.

"*Um*," she said. And then, still squeaking, "My father?"

"Bingo," said Pedro.

"How did you know?"

"It's obvious."

"How?"

"Because, whenever you are playing, and he walks by, you're playing gets a little worse."

"Not better?"

"Worse. You're trying to make it better, sure. But you start to strain, you stiffen up, and the notes aren't quite the same. It's hard to describe, but it happens. Every time."

"*Every* time?"

"Well, almost every time."

"Wow," said Erica.

"I'm not blaming you," Pedro said. "Your father doesn't look happy to me."

Erica frowned. "He's not," she said. "Although, for a while he seemed a little better, after those St. Bernards jumped all over him. But that didn't last."

"How come?" said Pedro. "What makes him sad?"

"I wish I knew," said Erica. "Sometimes I think he really doesn't want to be a college professor. I don't know if he knows what he wants."

"But you can't fix that," Pedro said. "That's my point. Those St. Bernards might show up once in a while out of the blue, or out of the privy, but there's nothing you can do to arrange that, is there?"

"No," she said, shaking her head. "There's not."

A small hush settled between them, still filled with the wind and the rain.

"So now we're even," she finally said.

"Even, Steven," Pedro said.

"Hey," said Erica. "That sounds kind of dumb."

"Good," said Pedro. "I was trying for dumb. Thought I could impress you that way."

"Oh," said Erica, "I'm very impressed!" And she put her hand atop his again, and they intertwined their fingers like the fresh notes to a madrigal.

"You can play your music for me whenever you want, Erica," Pedro said. And now it was his voice that was squeaking. "But I want you to play for yourself. I want you to play for you. That's what I want you to do."

Erica felt herself smile. "Sayest thou so?" she asked.

"In sooth," he said. "In simple sooth."

And that is when they tried their first kiss. As they sat at ease.

A Note about the Past

HENGRAVE HALL LIES JUST NORTH OF the town of Bury St. Edmunds in Suffolk. Little is known about Queen Elizabeth's visit to Hengrave in late August of 1578. One brief account mentions "a shew representing the Phayries (as well as might be)," during which "a rich jewell was presented to the Queenes Highnesse." She was well feasted, and chose to grant a knighthood to Thomas Kytson in spite of his Catholic leanings. He must have been rather nervous, since his Catholic neighbor Master Rokewood, ten miles away in Thetford, had days earlier lost his house and freedom to the Queen's displeasure.

Whether Margaret and Mary Kytson played the virginal for the Queen is unknown, but it would have been common for the young daughters of country houses to entertain an important visitor in this way. The Kytson sisters were given lessons, perhaps from the composer-in-residence Edward Johnson, and Queen Elizabeth liked to surprise her courtiers by displaying her skill on the virginal at odd moments. "All in a Garden Green" was a favorite song in the court of Elizabeth and also in the court of her father, Henry VIII. (The lute song performed at the banquet also dates from the time of Henry VIII; it is called "My lute, awake!" and was written by Sir Thomas Wyatt the Elder.)

Margaret really did marry Charles Cavendish through the conniving of his mother, Bess of Hardwick, a powerful and greedy woman. And once married, she did perish in childbirth at an early age. Her sister Mary lived to be 80. Through Mary, nine more generations—all of them Catholic—occupied Hengrave Hall until the family disappeared at the end of the nineteenth century.

For a number of decades Hengrave served as a Catholic school for girls, then as a retreat center graciously hosted by the Sisters of the Assumption. Since 2006, Hengrave Hall has been privately owned, and is now used for grand weekend wedding parties. The QE Chamber is the bridal suite.

Acknowledgments

MY FIRST AND ONLY VISIT TO HEN-
grave was in the autumn of 1992, when my
wife and son and daughter and I accompa-
nied a group of students for a fall semester of study. At
the time, I wasn't so sure I really wanted to be a teacher,
and it showed. Afterward, I wanted to repair the experi-
ence by thinking what it might have been like to come to
Hengrave as a child, or at least as a younger person. I want
to thank Sister Jill of the Sisters of the Assumption for
sharing both her personal wisdom and some of the history
of Hengrave. My teaching assistant at the time, Laurie
Camp, now Laurie Camp Hatch, also kept me attuned to
the history of the place, insisting, as she did, on sleeping
in the one room that even the nuns regarded as haunted.

After our visit I learned many things from a book
published in 1822 by the antiquarian John Gage, *The
History and Antiquities of Hengrave in Suffolk*. I also cor-
responded with the very helpful present-day antiquarian
of Hengrave, Alan Merryman.

Once the story was drafted, I benefited from the
comments of many readers and listeners. Among them
were Paul Delaney, David Downing, Michelle Drake,

Acknowledgments

Tracy Groot, Elizabeth Hess, Catherine Abbey Hodges, Sara Johnson, Bill Jolliff, Bethany Marroquin, Marilyn Chandler McEntyre, Barb Pointer, Tom Schmidt, Mark Eddy Smith, Heather Speirs, Greg Spencer, Dan Taylor, and John Wasson. I am especially grateful for the final guidance of my Slant editor, Gregory Wolfe, and for release time from my courses at Westmont College, generously provided by my provost, Mark Sargent. Of course, I also want to thank my wife, Sharon, and our two children, Jonathan and Hanna, for allowing and supporting my immersion in this tale. *Bon temps viendra.*

This book was set in Adobe Garamond Pro and IM Fell English, the latter typeface being named after John Fell (1625–1686), Bishop of Oxford and one of the founders of Oxford University Press. Fell's efforts helped to create a distinctively British tradition of typography.

This book was designed by Mike Surber, Ian Creeger, and Gregory Wolfe. It was published in hardcover, paperback, and electronic formats by Wipf and Stock Publishers, Eugene, Oregon.

The cover design incorporates a depiction of Hengrave Hall (in the lid of the virginal) and a portrait of Queen Elizabeth I of England known as "The Ermine Portrait" (1585) by Nicholas Hilliard and held in the collection of Hatfield House, Hatfield, England.